Sherlock Holmes
and
A Quantity of Debt

From the Notebooks of
Dr. John H. Watson, M.D.

By
David Marcum

Paperback ISBN 9781780924991
ePub ISBN 9781780925004
PDF ISBN 9781780925011

Published in the UK by MX Publishing
335 Princess Park Manor, Royal Drive,
London, N11 3GX

www.mxpublishing.co.uk
Cover design by www.staunch.com

For Rebecca and Dan
As Always and Forever

Editor's Introduction

I t was a dark and stormy afternoon . . . .

I recall it vividly, that afternoon when I really first encountered Mr. Sherlock Holmes of Baker Street. It was in the summer of 1975, I was ten years old, and some weeks (or months – who knows at this point?) earlier, I had acquired my first Holmes volume. I hadn't really wanted it at the time, so it had been put on a shelf for unloved books.

On that particular and wonderful afternoon, a very rainy and dark Saturday, we were sitting around the house, my mother, my sister, and myself. I'm not sure where my dad was at the time, so he wasn't present at my epiphany. (I recently asked my sister, and she doesn't remember the event, but I do.) The room was dark, with the only glow coming from the television. That was unusual, because we usually had the lights on. The darkness reflected the grim boredom of the whole day.

Back then, there were only three channels on the television. I stood up and walked across the room in order to try to find something better than whatever we were watching — there were no remote controls in our house in those days — and came across *A Study in Terror* (1965), starring John Neville as Holmes, and Donald Houston as Watson.

Of course, I didn't know what movie it was then, or who the actors were. It would be years before I would find the film again and be able to watch it in its entirety. But somehow, even in my ignorance on that day, I knew that this was Holmes. Don't ask me how. I had never read a Holmes story or seen a Holmes movie at that point. Maybe it was just an awareness of who Holmes was, the same amazing thing that makes him one of the most recognizable figures in the world. More likely, it was simply that fact that the speakers referred to the main character as *Sherlock* and *Holmes.*

In any case, it was the scene where Mycroft, played by Robert Morley, comes to call and squabble with our hero. The quick dialogue, and possibly even the bright colors of the 1960's film, somehow appealed to me. During a commercial, I ran back to my room and found the then-single Holmes volume — I still have it — in my eventually massive collection and brought it back with me for further study. It didn't take long to read the nine stories in that book.

It all tumbled after that. I sought out more tales of the Canon. I borrowed ahead on my allowance and purchased the complete Doubleday edition. At Christmas, my parents presented me with Baring-Gould's *Sherlock Holmes of Baker Street*, and I had really found the door into Holmes's world.

Not long after that, Nicholas Meyer, who had started the great 1970's Holmes resurgence with his novel *The Seven-Per-Cent Solution*, published the follow-up, *The West End Horror* (1976). This was the first truly great non-Canon tale that I had ever read. (Strangely, it is often mistakenly referred to as a Holmes-versus-The Ripper tale. However, it is set in 1895, not 1888, and involves the murder of actors and critics in the West End, and not the poor Whitechapel victims. I highly recommend it, nearly forty years after I first read it, and I was fortunate enough to say the same thing to Mr. Meyer in late 2011, when I got to meet him at a Sherlockian gathering in Bloomington, IN.)

In Meyer's introduction, he relates how, after the publication of *The Seven-Per-Cent Solution*, he received a number of newly discovered Watson manuscripts from various sources. Some were obvious forgeries, but not all of them.

I had a similar experience after the publication of my recent books, *The Papers of Sherlock Holmes*. After many kind comments, (and a few wondering why the books weren't about Cumberbatch and Freeman's "Sherlock" and "John"), I received a cryptic email with a single PDF image of a handwritten page containing Watson's handwriting.

I can't tell you much more than that. After some back-and-forth communications, it was arranged that the following narrative from Watson's journals could be published. I had been prepared to beg and plead, and perhaps take a second mortgage on my house, in order to obtain the manuscript, but the mysterious owner, who insists on anonymity, had wanted all along to make sure that the story was told. I have the impression that there are personal motivations and perhaps some old grudges involved, but I have no knowledge of any specifics.

I was glad to see that the manuscript seemed to confirm some of the information about Watson's *first* wife, as detailed in Baring-Gould's *Sherlock Holmes of Baker Street,* which has meant so much to me over the years. As was the case with *The Papers of Sherlock Holmes,* any misunderstandings of the contents of Watson's smudged journal and rather cramped handwriting must be blamed on my editing and not on the good Doctor.

And also, as I did with the previous volumes, I wish to dedicate the effort involved in preparing this manuscript to both my wife Rebecca, with much love for her patience and support regarding my fascination with the world of Holmes and Watson, and my also my son Dan, best friend and patient listener to my wound-up ramblings. Thank you both for everything!

DAVID MARCUM

August 7th, 2013
The 161st Anniversary of the Birth of Dr. John H. Watson

The illustration by Frank Wiles (on the opposite page) is from the epilogue to The Valley of Fear *(1915), and shows Inspector MacDonald in Holmes and Watson's sitting room in early March 1888, approximately one month before the events of this volume . . . .*

Inspector MacDonald nodded. "It is a case of murder. But," he added, dramatically lowering his voice, "it seems to be a murder from the days of our grandparents!"

"So now, as an infallible way of making little ease great ease, I began to contract a quantity of debt."

— Pip in **Great Expectations**
by Charles Dickens

Chapter 1 – A Baker Street Visitor

"I should not be so inclined," stated Mr. Sherlock Holmes, from his stool at the chemical table in the corner.

I roused myself from the brown study into which I had fallen as the morning progressed. With a sigh, I pulled my gaze from the rain-streaked windows and back to Holmes. "And to what would you be referring?" I asked.

Holmes did not speak for a moment, as he leaned closer to the elaborate glass apparatus before him, titrating some violet-colored liquid between the interconnected pieces of narrow tubing. He placed his eyes level with the thin vertical structures, clamped in place above the blue gas flame that flickered across his sharp features. I started to utter a warning, afraid the collar of his dressing gown would touch the flame, but it proved to be unnecessary. Then, satisfied with the results, Holmes leaned back, stretching like a cat, and shifted to face me.

"I would not be inclined to record the events of the last couple of days in your journals. Our recent trip to Kent* is hardly worth preserving for posterity. The matter was simple child's play, and was quickly resolved by means of a single telegram to my professional contacts in Ohio. It really is not worth the effort that would be expended in adding it to your notes."

I straightened in my chair. "I must disagree, Holmes. Your analysis of the matter was masterful, you brought peace of mind to that unhappy young man, and – incidentally – you did capture a murderer."

Holmes turned back toward his research, leaned toward the

_____

*See "The Singular Affair at Sissinghurst Castle" in *The Papers of Sherlock Holmes*, edited by David Marcum, 2011, 2013 deal table, and reached for his pen. With his left hand, he pulled a sheet of paper toward him, already half-covered with cryptic notes. "Nevertheless . . . ."

My thoughts that morning had indeed touched upon the events of the previous day in Kent, and the audacious scheme the wily American had planned there. If Holmes and I had not been summoned, doubtless the fellow would have accomplished his goals and escaped unscathed.

But I had been having other thoughts as well, more personal and grim than just the facts relating to our recent investigation. Perhaps Holmes realized that, and had chosen to direct the conversation toward my literary efforts, rather than let me brood, as had been my habit the last few months. Or possibly Holmes did not realize the true path of my thoughts at all. But knowing Holmes, that was unlikely indeed.

I shook my head, and tried to turn my thinking to other matters, but as I glanced around the sitting room, so filled with souvenirs and relics from Holmes's past investigations, I realized that very little of my own possessions were in evidence. It had only been a little over one hundred days since I had returned to Baker Street, and I wondered if it was time for me to think about getting back into harness and finding a new practice. How different were those one hundred days from what I had planned for the rest of my life! And how different would the next hundred be, and the hundred after that?

I decided to respond to Holmes's query, out of politeness, if for no other reason. If he had actually made an effort to distract me, as he had done so often since the events of last December, I was obliged to return his volley, if only out of friendly gratitude for the trouble that he was taking, such as it was. I looked back at the pile of newspapers littering our dining table, souvenirs of our most recent investigation. They had drawn my attention all morning. "And how," I asked, "did you know that I was thinking of our recent trip to Sissinghurst?"

Holmes patiently stilled the pen for just a moment, but did not turn to face me. "It took no deduction, I assure you," he replied, and then recommenced writing in his careful precise way. "After you finished your breakfast, you carried the mementos of our investigation to the table, and then you moved to your desk, where you stood for some three-and-a-half minutes, running your fingers over your journals while eventually declining to actually pick one up."

"You could tell that from just listening?" I interrupted.

"You were, after all, right behind me. And I've heard the sound before. You then paced back to the table, opened some of the newspapers related to the Sissinghurst matter before laying them back down. Then, returning to your chair, empty-handed I might add, you have spent the rest of the time sighing at regular intervals as you attempted to find the will to start recording the matter. Finally, I decided to assist you in your decision by offering my opinion."

"I did not realize that even the sounds I make are so predictable, or distracting – "

"Do not trouble yourself, Watson. Luckily, my research here requires no great amount of concentration, and I was in no way distracted from reaching the correct conclusion."

"And you do not think that recording yesterday's events is a worthwhile activity on this rainy morning?" I asked.

"It is of no concern to me," Holmes replied, only to immediately contradict himself by stating, "However, if your narrative is to be presented in any way similar to that melodrama that was foisted upon the unsuspecting public last Christmas . . . . " His voice trailed off, as everything that he had to say had already crossed my mind, and my answer had crossed his.

We had been down this road before. I was weary of trying to convince Holmes that, while his accounts should be shared with the public, they must be presented in such a way that the public would actually *want* to read them. If Holmes had his way, my recently published narrative, constructed with all the respect and admiration that I could put into it, would have appeared in some scholarly journal, perhaps *The Lancet*, detailing in a detached and clinical fashion the procedure for determining which of two identical water-soluble pellets contained a fast-acting poison, while never mentioning the dramatic events stretching across two continents that would lead one to the manufacture of those deadly objects in the first place.

"I see," I replied, refusing to rise to the occasion, and glancing once more at the papers littering our dining table. I did not feel like fighting that battle yet again, on that dark morning, and I did not say anything else as he adjusted the sheet of paper on the scarred tabletop and continued to write.

A particularly strong gust of wind threw the heavy rain against our window, pulling my mind away from the disagreement. The past couple of days had been beautiful, with the promise of spring showing strongly. But as we were returning from Kent the previous evening, the skies had opened and poured forth a veritable deluge that seemed to have settled in for the duration. It had rained throughout the night, and the morning skies had revealed themselves to be filled with heavy, ominous clouds. Even with the currently heavy rain, there was a sense of impending tension, as if the next wave of something worse might begin at any moment.

There had been some talk the previous day, as we set out for our return to London, of the two of us going to the British Museum in the morning, in order to view a singular treasure that had ended up there many years ago, following one of Holmes's early investigations in central Norfolk. Holmes had told me the matter had some similarities to the events just resolved at Sissinghurst. However, when I had descended from my room that morning, Holmes had been busy at the chemical table, and no further mention was made of the outing. I found I rather felt like a petulant child, deprived of a trip to the zoo because his papa unexpectedly has chosen to work instead.

Holmes continued to scribble for another moment before flinging down his pen and then springing to his feet, bellowing

4

for Mrs. Hudson as he moved across the sitting room, the paper waving in his hand.

Throwing open the door to the landing, he again cried, "Mrs. Hudson!"

I heard the footsteps of our long-suffering landlady start up the steps. At exactly that moment, the front doorbell rang. She paused for an instant, as if undecided which way to turn, and then I heard her move off the steps and down the hall in order to answer the door. Holmes snorted impatiently from the open doorway and then walked to the fireplace, side-stepping the sturdy basket chair in his path that was usually reserved for visitors. He reached to the mantle for his cherry pipe, which he smoked when in a disputatious mood, and began to pack it with his strong shag tobacco, kept in a Persian slipper tacked to the side of the mantelpiece.

He had successfully lit the pipe, and was smoking and drumming his fingers on the mantle when Mrs. Hudson appeared in the sitting room doorway. Holmes looked over at her, stated "Ah!" and crossed the room with his quick decisive footsteps. "No need to wait in the hall, Mr. Mac," he said. "Come in! Come in!"

Mrs. Hudson moved aside, allowing the tall figure of Inspector Alec MacDonald to enter the room. He nodded, first to me, and then to Holmes. I was surprised, as I had only heard Mrs. Hudson coming up the steps, but then the Inspector was always a canny fellow, and I'm sure he had matched his steps to those of our landlady, perhaps seeing if he could get one over on Holmes.

When I first came to live in Baker Street, initially as a wounded war veteran without friend or kin in England, and began sharing rooms with the strange young man recently introduced to me as Sherlock Holmes, I had no idea what his chosen place in life actually was. Over the course of those first few months, I knew that Holmes was often consulted by a number of unusual individuals, including many I later learned were Scotland Yard Inspectors. Initially, they seemed embarrassed to seek out Holmes's services, or even resentful. They certainly attempted either to claim credit outright for Holmes's efforts in providing them with a solution, or more often, deluded themselves into thinking that they had actually figured things out on their own, with some small assistance from the unofficial consulting detective.

But as time moved on, I began to see a change in the way that Holmes was treated by the official force, subtle at first, but later quite obvious. Holmes's opinion was respected without reservation, and many was the time that a Yarder beat a path to our door with something unusual, because they had come to learn that Holmes craved the *outré* in the same way a prisoner craves freedom. As the respect, and I will have to say the friendship as well, grew between Holmes and the Inspectors of the Yard, one could see that they too enjoyed being able to bring something unique to offer to the Master. Inspectors Gregson and Lestrade, of course, had finally come around, along with Lanner, Youghal, and Bradshaw soon after. Peter Jones was much quicker to offer overtures of actual friendship and respect toward Holmes than was his brother and fellow Inspector, Athelney. But the first Inspector that truly seemed to appreciate Holmes, not just as a useful tool toward clearing his caseload, but rather as a friend, was Alec MacDonald. And I, who had watched this process for a number of years, was glad to see it.

"Gentleman," MacDonald said, with his soft Scots burr, "'tis not a fit day to be out, I know, but I'm afraid that I'm requesting your company."

Holmes cocked his head and raised a questioning eyebrow. He took a deep pull on his pipe, as he seemed to ask without words, "Well?"

Inspector MacDonald nodded. "It is a case of murder. But," he added, dramatically lowering his voice, "it seems to be a murder from the days of our grandparents!"

"Excellent," replied Holmes, with a nod. "Just the thing."

6

Holmes glanced to the left, toward Mrs. Hudson, who was gathering up the cold coffee pot and cups from breakfast. He stepped in her direction, the paper he had been holding thrust out toward her. "Mrs. Hudson, please have the boy dispatch this telegram immediately."

With a tolerant smile, and an additional glance toward me, she took the paper, laid it among the coffee detritus, and said, "Will you have time for some more coffee, or tea, before you have to leave?"

Holmes looked toward MacDonald, who answered, with his accent suddenly thicker than I had ever heard it, "Ah believe 'at we hae th' time. An' frae a body Scot tae anither, Mrs. Hudson, Ah cannae hink ay anythin' 'at Ah woods loch better."

Hearing him speak in such a thick dialect, I was reminded of my own father, and my childhood in Stranraer. I suddenly realized that Holmes was greatly outnumbered by Scots, and I likewise whimsically considered having a go at saying something in my boyhood accent. Mrs. Hudson simply smiled and nodded, and then turned to go, carefully pulling the door shut behind her. I wondered if it did her good to hear the sounds of her homeland.

MacDonald moved into the room, heading toward the basket chair centered before the warm fire. He had been there many times before when seeking Holmes's counsel. "Such a spring," he muttered, sounding again like the more familiar Alec MacDonald. He sat down and simultaneously leaned forward, large hands outstretched. His damp boots matted the bear skin rug underneath his feet. "Beautiful weather we've had for the last two days, and now this," he muttered. "Such a spring," he repeated.

Holmes had also moved to his chair. Seating himself, he arranged his dressing gown around him and asked, "And where will you be requiring us today, MacDonald?"

"Three miles back this side of Woburn," MacDonald replied, "out in Bedfordshire." Then something seemed to

7

occur to him. "That is, unless you're already involved in something else? I apologize. I hope – "

"As a matter of fact, we did just return from Kent, where our most recent investigation – " I said, observing with a sour eye that the rain running down the window glass, looking out onto Baker Street, now seemed to be heavier than before.

Holmes interrupted me. " – But we are currently free at the moment to assist you, Mr. Mac. And in any event, our journey to Kent *wasn't* technically my most recent investigation," he said. "I've since been consulted on another matter following our return to London yesterday, and having just concluded that case as well – "

"Concluded it?" I asked. "When? Did it involve the chemical experiment that you just completed?"

"As I was saying," Holmes continued, "having just concluded that matter, I believe a trip to the countryside around Woburn will satisfactorily fill our time."

"But what of the chemical experiment?" I asked. "I had believed you were simply carrying out some test or other as a way to pass your time on such a rainy day."

"Not at all, Watson," Holmes replied. "I received information for which I had been waiting just this morning, before you arose. It came in the form of a wire from Lestrade, concerning the little matter of the fourth clerk, as was described to us so vividly last week."

"Ah," said MacDonald. "Concerning the Titian Oils?"

"Quite." Holmes glanced at the mantle clock. "Tell me, do we have time for this discussion, or should we be making preparations for departure?"

MacDonald also looked at the clock, and then pulled out his watch for comparison. Apparently satisfied, he returned the watch to its pocket and stated, "We have enough time, and to spare. You will both be able to make ready, and I will be able to enjoy some of Mrs. Hudson's fine coffee. Then we will set out on our expedition to reach Euston. And," he said, with a rueful grin in my direction, "perhaps – although I don't really believe it – *perhaps* the rains will have departed by the time we are ready to go."

"Not likely," I said, grimly. Sitting up straighter in my comfortable chair, I asked, "What is this about, MacDonald? Murder, I believe you said?"

"Ah, there's plenty of time to discuss it on the train," he said, the grin sliding off his face. "I will tell you, however, that it involves the Briley family of Bedfordshire, and the discovery of an old corpse, more of a mummy really, in a most unusual place. And Mr. Holmes, the dead man has *a missing little finger on his right hand!*"

MacDonald made his final statement with lowered voice and an ominous overtone, but the significance of the statement completely escaped me. Of what importance was a missing finger on a desiccated corpse?

In contrast to my confusion, Holmes's eyes seemed to focus more sharply for just an instant with understanding, and then he slightly relaxed, although only in a way that someone who had known him for so long would recognize. "This does seem to promise to be of some interest," he said. I started to ask in what way, but MacDonald interrupted me.

"Right now, however, I'd dearly love to hear about Mr. Holmes's discovery related to Mr. Lestrade's investigation. Am I to understand that you have solved it, then?"

Holmes had been working to relight his pipe, which, in this damp weather, was resisting him. Seemingly frustrated for the moment, he paused and stated, "That particular storm seems to have broken, so to speak, last night, when the villain in question finally lost his patience and acted indiscriminately. Lestrade's men were watching as I'd advised, and they were able to take the samples as I had requested. Lestrade arrived before daybreak this morning, knocking Mrs. Hudson up. She proceeded to do the same to me. After studying the samples that Lestrade had obtained, I compared one in particular to the different fluids previously found at the scene, and determined through my analysis that the poison could only have been placed there by Brooks. That was what was written in the wire I just sent out with Mrs. Hudson. As you can see, there was really no taxing effort involved at all, and I am now quite fully rested. As I hoped you were too, Watson."

He finally gave up trying to light his pipe and laid it aside. "Will we be traveling to Leighton, then?"

MacDonald nodded. "And then on by carriage, I'm afraid. Four miles. But it's just as bad to go past and work our way back and around from Stratford."

Mrs. Hudson chose that moment to enter with the coffee and fresh cups. MacDonald stepped up to help her, and I stood to join them, as I wished to fortify myself before beginning our journey.

"As I recall," said Holmes, clearly indifferent to the call of the hot, dark brew, "the Euston train to Leighton leaves within the hour. I suggest that we depart on time, in case the weather conspires to delay us."

He stood, and started to walk toward his room, shedding his dressing gown as he went. "Should we plan for an overnight sojourn, MacDonald?"

MacDonald, trying to blow on the coffee in order to cool it, stopped long enough to reply, "It probably couldn't hurt, Mr. Holmes. I'm not sure to what extent this affair will stretch. They have certainly uncovered a mess out there. Literally uncovered, as you shall see."

Seeing that I also held a cup of coffee, and was returning to my chair by the fire, Holmes paused on the way to his room and asked, "Am I to understand, then, that you do not wish to accompany us, Watson, and rusticate in Bedfordshire, in order to recover from our outing yesterday to the Kent countryside?"

With a snort, I stopped before pausing beside my chair and raised the coffee to my lips. Forgetting MacDonald's example, I nearly touched my lips to it before remembering its scalding power. Placing it on the small table by my chair, I said, "Never fear, Holmes, I will answer the call."

I started for the sitting room door, intending to go upstairs to my bedroom. I kept a traveling kit there, ready for just such excursions as these. With an abrupt and knowing "Ha!" Holmes continued into his room.

Within just a few minutes, my preparations were complete. Placing my bag by the sitting room door, I crossed to my chair and picked up the cup. The coffee was now at just the right temperature, and in a few sips it was gone. MacDonald was finishing his, and he looked longingly at the pot on the table. But he reluctantly set his cup aside, and we made to leave, moving around one another near the door as we retrieved coats and hats.

As we started down the steps, MacDonald in front of us, Holmes gripped my shoulder and murmured, "After all, Watson, work *is* the best antidote." With an additional squeeze, he released me and moved downstairs behind the Inspector. I shifted my bag from my right hand to my left, gripped the rail, and realized that Holmes had probably divined the nature of my thinking while he conducted his chemical analysis.

I found that I had to agree with him. I had discovered during the early part of that year, and on into the spring, that assisting in Holmes's investigations had indeed helped to heal me from my grief during the previous Christmas season. I only hoped that the matter which had now captured our attention would also prove to distract me from my sad thoughts earlier that morning.

Chapter 2 – Out To Bedfordshire

Fifteen minutes later, we were in a four-wheeler, flying toward Euston Station. I realized that Holmes was displaying extraordinary patience as he waited to hear the details of the murder near Woburn. I wished to know more about the cryptic statement concerning the Briley family and the corpse's missing little finger. Before we had departed the sitting room, Holmes had briefly examined the "B" volume of his massive index before closing it with a resounding snap and dropping it on the settee. He had then seemed more eager than ever to begin our next investigation.

I was also looking forward to hearing about it, and I knew we would have plenty of time on the journey to sort out the reasons behind our summons. I shifted in my seat, and felt the comfortable lump of my old service revolver in my topcoat pocket. In the early days, Holmes would often have needed to specifically remind me to bring it. I had long since learned not to leave home without it. Beside me, Holmes focused off into the distance, his nostrils twitching as if he were already catching the scent of whatever trail was waiting for us.

He remained silent but tense, like a coiled spring, until the four-wheeler turned in to the bustle and noise of Euston Station. With a bound, Holmes leapt to the ground, tossing some coins to the driver, while I made to follow as best as I could.

We made our way into the station and through the crowds to the correct train. MacDonald had anticipated our agreement to his request and had already arranged for a First Class Smoker. After we were settled in and the train began its first lurchings toward departure, Holmes, who had possessed himself in a patient state for long enough, said, "And now, Mr. Mac, tell us more about the mysterious corpse and the Briley family."

MacDonald, in the process of lighting his pipe, was not to be rushed. Seeing this, Holmes decided to join him, pulling out his old oily, black clay pipe, which he often used while traveling. After they had both gone through the comforting rituals of preparation, and after I had declined both their offers to join them, MacDonald was finally ready to speak.

"I could see," he began, "that my mention of the Briley family and the missing little finger seemed familiar to you, Mr. Holmes."

"Indeed," replied Holmes. "I recalled something of the family characteristic, and a review of my index confirmed it."

"Well, I don't know anything about it," I interrupted, finding I was still in a somewhat surly mood, "so please enlighten me." Hearing how my voice had sounded, I resolved to moderate it in the future.

"Certainly," said Holmes. "Living in Bedfordshire, nearer Woburn than Leighton for more years than I know, has been the Briley family. The family's great wealth has been matched only by their odd stand-offishness. They have always maintained a successful estate, but have never shown interest in journeying to London for the season, or currying favor with the Royal Court. In short, they have maintained their affairs for several generations, conserving their resources, and generally staying out of the public eye."

"And the intriguing business of the missing finger?" I asked.

"There is a Briley family trait," said MacDonald, "that generally manifests itself, for generation after generation in the male line of the family. Briley boys are always born with a missing little finger on their right hand."

"What?" I said. "Surely such things would occur on both hands, and not just one. And it would have been bred out of the family by now."

"Not necessarily, Watson," said Holmes. "Consider some of the other unique traits that run through different families. Royal families, for instance, often display characteristics that become well-known. Our own Queen's children and grandchildren have had to face the possibility of hemophilia with each new generation of births. And of course, there is the unfortunate Hapsburg Lip or Jaw. I'm afraid the idea of a congenital missing finger is not at all inconceivable."

He looked back at MacDonald. "And in what way is a missing little finger related to a corpse? Is it somehow connected to Martin Briley, the current head of the family, who, if I am correct, is in his sixties and in poor health?"

"You are certainly correct about Mr. Briley," replied MacDonald. "But it is not his missing finger to which I refer. When I left there late last night, Mr. Briley was still alive, and he is certainly not the dead man in question. No, the corpse to which I refer was uncovered in a workman's trench on the property, and appears to have been buried there for nearly fifty years!"

"And it is missing a finger? The little finger on its right hand?" said Holmes. "Are you implying that it is a family member whose body has been concealed for nearly half a century?"

"I am, Mr. Holmes. That's what makes it a delicate situation, and that's the truth. You can see why I asked for your help, and that of the doctor."

"I begin to perceive your dilemma," said Holmes.

"And that dilemma would be?" I asked.

Holmes shifted his pipe, and said, "In a case such as this, one must be careful about ruffling the feathers of someone as wealthy as Martin Briley. He has a reputation of being a good man, although he tends to keep strictly to himself. He has spent a lifetime making the area around his estate a better place for all who work and live there, at no little expense to himself. In some ways, he has lived his life as something of a benevolent king of his own little fiefdom. But," he added, "it is always a treacherous path when someone in the Inspector's position has to rake up old family skeletons. In this case, literally."

"You're right, Mr. Holmes. The local constable instantly saw the implications of finding a long-buried and possibly unknown Briley, and called me in. Now it's become my problem, and I'm hoping you will see a way to a solution that might be outside of my means."

Holmes took a deep draw on his pipe and said, "Begin at the beginning." And he closed his eyes to listen.

MacDonald took a deep breath and spoke.

"Several months ago, the estate agent, George Burton, began a series of long-overdue repairs. Burton, a man of about thirty years, grew up on the estate, and had an eye for what needed to be done. He said that Mr. Martin Briley was more than willing to fund the work, and left the matter completely in Burton's hands as to what would and would not be fixed.

"Many of the repairs were routine, including painting the buildings where needed, reclaiming the old family mausoleum from the vegetation that was overtaking it, reworking some of the drainage around a mere on the property, and so on. One of the jobs involved replacement of the drain tile that leads away from a series of cottages that had been built for the estate workers back in the 1820's. The pipe to be replaced leads from these buildings down a long hill, where it empties into the mere. Burton told me the cottages are on a part of the estate that retained water in times past, apparently due to the rocky geology at the top of the hill where they were built. Several people had gotten sick in the old days, before the drains were installed. Or at least Burton says they had. He couldn't know himself for certain, as he is far too young. Burton says the old estate records show that the pipes were first installed in 1840. In recent years, the drains have started to clog, and Burton finally instituted repairs before things could get any worse.

"Two days ago, on the fourteenth, workmen were digging down to replace the line from the cottages to the mere. They had been working on that particular job for several weeks, starting at the top of the hill near the cottages, and moving downhill. On that day, they routinely uncovered a section of clay pipe that had been buried there since the drains were installed, much like all the other pieces of pipe they saw as the repairs progressed. The ground around the excavation appears to be acidic it approaches the mere, and the ground has a certain peat-like quality to it, especially as it gets near to the water. That is important, as you shall see.

"As the workmen were digging around the existing pipe, they saw what appeared to be a leg sticking out from under it. Burton was called, and not long after, the local constable and a doctor. For several hours, the workmen slowly exposed the pipe, until they were able to carefully free the body.

"It was that of what seems to have been a young man, amazingly preserved, probably due to resting in the peat soil. He was wearing clothing from several generations back, matching the period when the pipe would have first been installed there."

"What was the condition of the ground at that location before any of the repairs began?" asked Holmes.

"You will be able to see for yourself," replied MacDonald, "but the foreman and the workers assure me that it was untouched. Nearby was a tree stump and roots that had been growing at that site up to the time the repairs had started there. I counted the tree's rings, and there were almost fifty clear ones, which means it probably started growing soon after the pipe was installed, forty-eight years ago. Part of the reason repairs were needed in that area was that some of the roots from the tree had worked their way into the clay pipe. If you're thinking that the body was placed there more recently, the evidence argues against it."

"Evidence can argue several ways, depending on the angle from which it is perceived," replied Holmes. "However, for the time being, I am willing to provisionally accept your theory that the body has been buried there since the installation of the pipe in 1840, pending the revelation of additional facts."

Settling back slightly, Holmes added, "To leap to the dramatic conclusion of your story, the body of the young man was missing the small finger of his right hand."

"Correct, Mr. Holmes," said MacDonald. "The body was incredibly well preserved, although there has obviously been some collapse of tissues, and the skin has browned from leaching fluids out of the peat soil. The hands were clenched, but were found to be still flexible, and they readily opened upon examination. The constable and the doctor immediately noticed the missing finger, but rightly did not announce the fact to the foreman or the workers. Recognizing the relationship between the missing finger and the Briley family, the constable wisely sent word to his superiors. Thus, my eventual involvement in the matter, and now yours.

"I traveled to Bedfordshire yesterday, in much better weather than we're seeing now, and on out to the estate, where I examined the excavation for myself. I'm convinced the location of the body has not been disturbed in the past half-century. I examined the hand with the missing finger with great care, and the deformity appears to be naturally occurring. There is no sign of a scar or past injury that would have accounted for the finger being lost after birth."

"But who could it be?" I interjected. "Is there some member of the Briley family that is unaccounted for?"

"I believe I can anticipate the Inspector's answer," stated Holmes. "From the notes in my index, I saw that the current Briley, Martin, is the last of the family, and was an only child. His father before him was also an only child. Therefore, there were no brothers or cousins extant from either Martin's or his father's generation."

"That we know of," I said.

"True," said MacDonald. "There could have been an illegitimate child with Briley blood that would have been the appropriate age in the late 1830's or early 1840's."

"Curious," said Holmes. "The body seems to have been hidden there from the time the pipe was first installed, in a

17

location that has remained undisturbed since then. The apparent dating of the clothing would tend to confirm this. The tree must have started growing around the late 1830's or early 1840's, if your count of nearly fifty rings is correct. And my research showed that the current head of the family, Martin Briley, came into his inheritance in 1840 as well, upon the death of his father, Galton Briley."

"Martin is still the head of the family, and the *last* head of the family," added MacDonald. "He has no children, and as far as I can determine, he has no heirs whatsoever. The estate is not entailed, and Briley has not publicly named who will succeed him when he dies. As his health is poor right now, and he is in his late sixties, the question is of some concern to the locals, who depend on the running and upkeep of the estate for their own livelihoods."

"What did Mr. Briley say when you questioned him about the corpse?" asked Holmes.

"Very little indeed," said MacDonald. "At first I had to pass the gauntlet of the man's harridan of a housekeeper, Mrs. Lynch. She gave me to understand in every possible way that the old man was too sick to receive visitors. The doctor was there, along with the local constable, and they were forced to concede that there was merit to the old woman's arguments.

"Finally, I was allowed to see him for ten minutes. He was in a corner of the library, in some sort of elaborate bath chair, bundled in blankets and placed near a roaring fire, as if he were unable to warm himself. I became quite uncomfortable in the short time I was there.

"He offered no information, except to say he hadn't any idea who it was that had been found, and there was no one at all that he could remember who might possibly be the body with the missing finger. Eventually he seemed to stop hearing me altogether and didn't respond any further to my questions.

"It was at that time, gentlemen, that Mrs. Lynch, who had hovered nearby throughout the entire interview, stepped in and informed me that I should leave. I did not feel I would make any further progress with the old man in any case, since he had stopped answering my questions, so I departed.

"I spent the rest of the day speaking with the various laborers who had helped uncover the corpse, and so on. You'll meet them yourself." Holmes nodded, and MacDonald continued. "At some point I realized I had already decided to seek your help, Mr. Holmes. And now, here we are, halfway to Bedfordshire."

"And that is probably a good place to stop," said Holmes. "Unless you have any additional pertinent information, we will be tempted to start speculating, and by the time we arrive at the estate, we will each have formed some theory or other in our minds that we will start trying to prove, bending what facts we find to fit our construct, instead of weighing each new revelation on its own merit.

"As you say," Holmes added, "I will wish to meet with these people myself when we arrive. Until that time, I beg of you not to speak until I've smoked a pipe or two while I arrange my thoughts."

As Holmes settled back to ponder what we had heard, I turned my attention from my companions inside of carriage and focused on the rainy, wet English countryside, visible through the window. The rain was streaking the glass, and I could only see bits and pieces of the passing landscape as we sped north toward Leighton, and then our ultimate destination, a few miles this side of Woburn. As the minutes moved by, I found myself settling back into the brown study of earlier that morning.

That spring of 1888 had been a difficult one for me, to say the least. I was not quite thirty-six years old, and I was at loose ends yet again. My original path, that of a military surgeon, had come to an abrupt end in 1880 on a hot Afghan battlefield. I had been fortunate enough to find a new purpose when I met my friend Sherlock Holmes half a year later. And then, after several years, I had perceived a new direction for my life, one I thought would last for the rest of my days. I had married and bought a practice, believing that I would live out my life as a husband, physician, and most certainly a father. But it was not to be.

The previous December, I had lost my wife, Constance, to a sudden illness. Tragically, we had only been married a little over a year at the time. I had met her in March 1885, during a period when I was living in San Francisco, attempting to rescue my brother from one of his spells of chronic drunkenness. I had gone to the western United States when my brother summoned me, in spite of the years of distance and disagreement between us. Holmes had advanced the funds for the journey without question, reaffirming to me — yet again — that he was more of a true brother than the actual one of my blood had ever been, or ever would be.

Arriving in San Francisco, I set out to make money in order to repay my brother's debts, and also what I now owed to Holmes, doing the only thing for which I was qualified. Establishing a small medical practice on Post Street, I was fortunate enough to receive as my first patient the lovely Miss Constance Adams.

Through a series of events that do not need to be recounted here, including a return to England later that year, and a subsequent visit back to the United States in early 1886, I realized that I wished to make Constance my own. In the spring of 1886, I returned to England, and Baker Street, for good, where I began to make plans to find a practice and a life I could share with my future wife.

As I recalled the promise of a life with my new bride, my thoughts were pulled for the moment back into the carriage, as Holmes was preparing to attempt to light his pipe. He was knocking the ash from the bowl against the window sill onto the floor below. After several sharp thuds, which did not seem to disturb the now-napping MacDonald in the least, Holmes was satisfied with his efforts, and he began to pack the bowl with the filthy shag that he favored. I smiled to myself and turned back toward the rain-streaked glass, letting my ruminations return to my dear departed wife.

Constance and I were married in late 1886, and we set up housekeeping in Kensington. My days were full and rewarding as we built the practice together. Like any newly married man, my interests turned inward toward hearth and home. And yet, I still found time to assist my best friend, Sherlock Holmes, on many of his investigations.

This arrangement seemed as if it would last indefinitely. However, I could not ignore the signs, as Constance appeared to weaken as 1887 progressed. She and her mother, who had journeyed to England with Constance before our marriage, tried traveling to various spas both around England and on the Continent in order to improve her condition, but all to no avail. I was forced to remain in London, as I continued to attempt to build up my practice by day, while by night I turned to writing to fill the empty hours.

Some time before, I had become acquainted with a fellow physician and aspiring writer named Conan Doyle. He had often tried to convince me to put some of Holmes's adventures down on paper, with an eye toward publication. I must confess that he did not have to urge me too strongly, since I already had the desire to do that very thing, and had felt that way since first observing Holmes in action in the Jefferson Hope matter, in 1881.

Doyle had long felt that I should either recount some of Holmes's cases, or perhaps even the events of my time in San Francisco. In fact, Doyle himself had tried to write his own version of some of the incidents from my California days, but when I saw what he had written, an awkward play entitled *Angels of Darkness,* I forbade him to continue, as some of the changes he made to the actual events were simply ludicrous.

During Constance's illness, Doyle's efforts began to wear me down, so that I finally agreed to write my own account of the Hope case, which was the first investigation that I ever shared with Holmes. Doyle himself wanted to write a portion

21

of the narrative providing background information relating to the events that led to the crime. When he was finished, I saw that he had incorporated portions of his aborted play, recounting some of my San Francisco days. After much disagreement, we agreed that his contribution could be included as written, in spite of several historical inaccuracies.

The narrative was finally published toward the end of 1887 in a cheap journal. I must admit that I was somewhat secretly disappointed, having pictured my hours of hard work finally appearing in something more substantial and permanent. Oddly, although my portion of the work clearly credited me with the segments that I had written, it was Doyle's name that appeared alone on the cover. However, I had no wish to seek literary fame, having only pursued the matter to make sure that Holmes's methods were brought to the attention of the public, and I did not seek to make any correction.

Two days after Christmas of 1887, I had stopped by Baker Street to present Holmes with a copy of the publication. His reaction, as might be expected, was — at best — not enthusiastic. I believe that he thought both Doyle and I had been preparing something that would be placed in a scientific journal.

Two days after my visit with Holmes, Constance unexpectedly died.

For a time, I was a man in a daze. Holmes took charge of everything, having served as best man at my wedding, and now as my best friend in my time of greatest need. He immediately invited me back to my old rooms in Baker Street. Within days, I agreed, having realized that I did not want to continue pursuing the practice I had been working so hard to build. It had never been very interesting or involving at the best of times, and I quickly sold it to escape from the unpleasant memories there. I was back in my old chair, before the fire in the sitting room, by the New Year.

New participation in Holmes's investigations had served as a useful distraction from my staggering loss. Already that year, both Holmes and I had been involved in numerous cases, including that of the Birlstone tragedy and puzzling brand discovered on the dead man's arm. The previous week Holmes and I had been down to Norbury, where he had identified the mysterious neighbor of Mr. Grant Munro, with whom I felt a special kinship, since both his wife and my deceased Constance were from America. It will be recalled that Holmes's prediction regarding the identity of Munro's neighbor was far more grim than the happy truth that was actually revealed.

As I had pondered over my journals that morning before MacDonald's arrival, I had considered adding the events of yesterday's journey to Kent. It would just fill the remaining space in the book, following the narrative concerning Munro, and Holmes's subsequent instructions to whisper "Norbury" into his ear if it should ever strike me that he was getting a little over-confident in his powers, or giving less pains to a case than it deserved.

My collection of notes regarding Holmes's adventures was growing impressively, and I considered whether I should eventually publish something else. If so, I did not know if I would involve Doyle in the process the next time. I felt I could do an adequate job on my own, both in terms of writing the pieces and having them published. And I had a wealth of information to choose from, including some adventures from Holmes's early days that he had only shared with me in recent months. Always very private in the past, he had become more open since Constance's death, talking about several of his earlier cases, such as that of the mysterious ritual of the Musgraves, as a way of distracting me from my recent bereavement.

I was pulled back from my wool-gathering by the arrival of the train in the station. No one spoke as we gathered our belongings and stepped out onto the platform. It was still raining steadily, and I pulled my coat tighter and settled my hat more firmly on my head.

Surrendering our tickets, we made our way outside and found one of the few carriages that would carry the three of us and the driver. "I'm afraid it's still a wee distance to the house," said MacDonald as we left the station.

There was no conversation during that miserable drive. Although it was April, my breath steamed in front of me, and occasionally a stray raindrop would work its way past my hat brim and down into my coat. It was hard to believe that only twenty-four hours earlier, it had been a beautiful spring day.

Finally, after I had lost track of time completely, the carriage turned, and the feel of the roadway changed. Looking up, I could see a large house, the features hidden in the mist and rain. It was two stories, and appeared to be in the shape of a shallow *U*, with the two wings on each side jutting toward us, and the wide base of the *U* set back in the middle. The carriage pulled to a stop across from the front door. The driver, who had not spoken throughout the entire journey, said in a gruff, little-used voice the only two words that I would hear him speak on the entire journey: "Briley House."

We had arrived at the scene of the crime.

Chapter 3 – On The Scene

Holmes glanced up at the dark clouds, seemingly unaware of the spray finding its way under the bill of his fore-and-aft cap. "I don't believe that the weather will improve," he said, "so perhaps we should see where the body was discovered before things get any worse."

"As you say, Mr. Holmes," agreed MacDonald. "Driver, take us down toward the mere, where the dead man was found."

With a nod, the driver gigged the horse, but almost immediately MacDonald exclaimed, "Stop!" Before the carriage had finished rolling, he leapt down to the ground, gathered our bags awkwardly in both hands, and ran to the door of the house, speaking for just a moment to the servant who had thrown open the door at our arrival. The fellow took the bags, nodded, and went back inside, closing the door behind him. MacDonald returned to the carriage and climbed in. "Now you can proceed," he stated.

Settling awkwardly into his seat as the vehicle began to move forward once again, MacDonald stated, "I told the man at the door to find George Burton and have him meet us where the body was found. I thought it would save us a little time out in the elements if he gets there a bit faster."

"Excellent thinking," I said, burrowing deeper into my coat, thankful for its bulk.

We returned to the small road in front of the house. The lane soon straightened out, its ruts filled with water. An open yard was on either side of us, which in the distance sloped down to a stream, spanned by a stone bridge. There were trees growing there, with one quite a bit taller than the others, serving as something of a border between the grounds of the large house and the small cluster of cottages perched on a hill on the other side of the churning stream.

As we descended the hill and crossed the bridge, I could see more of the homes used by members of the estate community. They were solid, square structures, built of local stone, and each with windows that glowed with warm light against the cold wet day. The smell of coal smoke was in the air, only slightly dampened by the rain. I knew that on a day like this, the fireplaces in the cottages were not likely to be drawing well.

Approaching the houses, I could see that they were laid out in a strict grid arrangement, with narrow lanes running between each row. There were probably fifty or more of the little buildings, and for all their similarity, I could also see individual touches, such as window boxes for herbs and flowers, and doors painted in different colors. There would certainly be more obvious differences, and I would have seen them, if only the light were better. But the day was dark, and seemed likely to stay that way.

Moving past the small cluster of houses, we left the road and continued on the slight slope down to where the stream appeared to curve back around the base of the hill. It widened, and while a clear movement of water could be seen drawing an open line down the center, the sides of the pond formed there were choked with reeds and other water grasses. A number of large trees grew along the perimeter of the mere, and off to our right, at the downstream end, was the carcass of one old giant elm that now lay on the ground, already sawn into several large pieces, its base and roots resting alongside a hole in the ground. There was a raw earthen line extending from that hole, back up the hill roughly parallel to our path down it, toward the houses now at our rear. This, then, was the path of the pipeline trench that had already been repaired.

The driver of the carriage was going slowly, in deference to the downward slope that we traversed, and the weight of a carriage with four grown men riding in it behind the single horse. He started bringing the animal to a stop well before our final destination. Setting the brake, he hopped down and walked to the horse's head. Taking her bridle, he rubbed her nose and made sure that she stayed in place while we stepped down.

Holmes darted ahead, looking into the hole, and then straightening up again. "It is as I feared," he said, gesturing to us when we joined him. The hole was filled with muddy water.

"Aye," agreed MacDonald. "There won't be anything to see in there for several days, and that's for sure."

"Then we will have to rely on your memory of what you saw on a brighter day," said Holmes, pulling his Inverness tighter as he finally appeared to acknowledge the weather.

MacDonald stepped to the lower rim of the hole, and gestured down. "You cannot tell it," he said, "but the trench contains a clay pipe of about one foot in diameter. This drains from the cottages up above, and into the lower end of the mere, where it is carried away by the stream.

"Of course, by the time I arrived, the body found here had already been removed. It seems that after the exposed leg was first seen, the hole was widened considerably, so that the workmen could gain access to the body. Dirt was also removed from underneath, and also from the other side of the pipe, so it could be taken out gently, and without fear of a cave-in. Only after it was out did they realize the body was in a more sturdy condition than they had first anticipated. Both the hole *and* the body were more sturdy," MacDonald added.

He gestured up the hill. "Right now, the fellow is up there, resting in an empty house. I had him left there, pending your examination, Mr. Holmes. It is locked, and seemed as good a place as any."

"Very good," said Holmes, glancing around. "And the tree? It was obviously growing at this location."

"Very near it, I'm told," nodded MacDonald, walking a step or two that way. "As you can see," he remarked, leaning over the stump, "the rings are quite defined, and easily count up to almost fifty. There are a few that are questionable on the outer side, near the bark, but it is certainly no older than that."

"I believe the rings are especially dark due to some aspect of the soil in this area," said a voice behind us.

We turned, to find a short fellow in his early thirties walking toward us. His face was hidden, as he was wearing very sturdy raingear, but almost immediately he pushed back his wide flat-brimmed hat, exposing a frank and open countenance. I had first thought that we had not heard him because of the masking sound of the rainfall, but I was to see later that he had a quiet step about him wherever he went.

"Inspector," he said, sticking out his hand toward MacDonald. "And this must be Mr. Holmes and Dr. Watson." He also shook our hands, his grip warm and dry, surprising on this damp cold day.

"George Burton," he said, as a fresh gust of wind spattered raindrops horizontally at us. "I'm Mr. Briley's agent."

"It is good to meet you," said Holmes. "I agree with you regarding the apparent properties of the soil. One would expect something of the sort in a lowland area such as this near a mere. What little examination I can make of the soil layers that have been exposed in the walls of the diggings seem to confirm the peat-like nature." Holmes patted one of the great sections of the trunk. "This was a tall tree."

"It was," said Briley. "A fine old English elm. It could even be seen from certain windows in the main house. I hated to have it cut down, but in order to repair this pipe, it had to go.

"When we started repairs on the estate several months ago, one of the items high on our list was improving the drainage from the cottages. These pipes were installed in 1840, according to the estate books, when Mr. Briley first inherited the place from his father. At that time, he instituted a number of continuing improvements, including this project, in order to better the quality of life for his workers. Sadly, the working lifespan of the pipes have reached their end, for the workers living above were starting to report unsanitary backups in the line.

"We decided to tie onto the existing outfall location at the top of the hill, where the smaller pipes from the various cottages collect and combine to exit the site. Then, digging down alongside the existing pipe, we replaced as we went. This old tree wasn't exactly on top of the pipes, but it was right beside them, and it was close enough that it had to go.

"We had gotten this far," he said, gesturing along the earthen line going up the hill, showing where the pipe trench had been dug and refilled, "before we found the body, day before yesterday."

"And you were not here when it was found?" asked Holmes.

"Correct," replied Burton. "Even though this was a crucial part of the repair, I was required at the main house just then, to take care of another matter."

"Why was this a crucial part?" asked MacDonald.

"The steeper angle of the pipe running off the hill changes around this point and flattens as it moves toward the final outfall," said Burton. "I wanted to make sure that the turn was accomplished successfully so the slope would be correct from here on out to the mere."

"Why were you following the path of the original pipeline?" asked Holmes. "Why not just make a new trench?"

"Geometry, Mr. Holmes. Just plain, simple geometry. The shortest distance between two points is a straight line, and all that. We knew that we wanted to start at the existing junction of pipes at the top of the hill, nearly five hundred feet from here, and to have our outfall at its same location at the optimum point of discharge at the downstream side of the mere. From the top of the hill, we followed the exact straight-line path that was used when the line was originally installed. To have found an alternate way would have extended the work, since the shortest path was the one that was originally taken, and would also have possibly impeded the flow in the pipe by putting an unnecessary curve or bend into the path of the pipe."

"I see," said Holmes. "Have you studied engineering, Mr. Burton?"

"Some, Mr. Holmes. When I was younger, Mr. Briley took an interest in me and saw that I had some tutoring. However, much of what I know now is just from simple experience, with a little common sense, and a willingness to admit what I don't know, and then to ask questions until I find out."

"Admirable, indeed," replied Holmes. He pointed to the tree stump and projecting roots. "I would guess that the stump was pulled out by a sturdy team?"

"That's right. We hitched them to the stump after the rest of the tree was cut down. As you might imagine, roots getting into a pipeline are a major source of blockage, and it would do us no good to replace the line through here without trying to slow or eliminate a large part of the problem."

"Quite." Holmes seemed to think a moment, and then, changing the subject, he asked, "Is the fact that the body was missing the little finger of the right hand still secret?"

MacDonald looked at Burton, who replied, "I believe so. I was notified of the discovery by one of the laborers. Lambrick, the man in charge. He knew nothing at that time except that the body had been found. I sent Lambrick with word for the constable and the doctor, and then came here. The body was still mostly covered at that point. When it was finally dug out enough to be pulled from underneath the pipe, it was quickly wrapped in a tarp for examination elsewhere.

"I had asked for the doctor and the constable to be discreet as they made their way down here, and it seems that no one up in the cottages was aware that anything out of the ordinary was taking place. We moved the body, and it was only upon later examination that we discovered the missing finger. The laborers had not seen it, and the constable and the doctor agreed that the knowledge should be kept to ourselves.

"It was then that the implications were fully realized, and the Constable decided that we should contact Scotland Yard."

Holmes nodded, glanced toward the carriage, and then up the hillside. "As much as I hate to suggest it, I believe that we should walk back up the hill in order to examine the body. I am afraid that if we all try to ride in the carriage, the poor beast will never be able get its footing to pull us back up." He looked toward me. "Will your leg stand it, Watson?"

I raised my cane and gave it a shake. "Lead on. Anything to get us out of this infernal rain for a few moments."

Luckily, no one fell as we struggled back up that five-hundred feet of wet grass, with its gentle but slick slope, toward the cottages. There were a few times, however, when it was a close thing. Finally we reached the flatter parts around the buildings, and stopped to get our breaths for a moment. Then, Burton led off between the cottages until coming to a stop beside one of the shabbier structures, its windows dark. MacDonald stepped up and, fishing a large old-fashioned key from his pocket, unlocked the door. He moved back out of the way as we stepped inside.

Burton moved to the left and in moments had first one, and then a second, lantern alight. The interior of the room was undecorated, the only furniture being a large and heavy deal table placed in the center of the room, symmetrical with a cold stone fireplace. Heavy curtains were pulled across the window, keeping the figure on the table hidden from curious passers-by.

"This seemed like a good place to store the body," said MacDonald, gesturing toward the sheeted object resting on the table. "It was standing empty.

"It's one of several houses that are scheduled for renovations," said Burton, indicating with his glance the run-down condition of the place. "We've left it untenanted after the most recent occupant departed, until we can make some repairs."

Holmes did not comment as he stepped quickly to the table. With a practiced flourish, he threw the sheet back to expose the body.

How to describe the horrid and macabre sight revealed there in that empty house, only poorly lit by the two flickering lanterns? It was the figure of a man, obviously, but twisted somewhat, and of a color that would not be natural, even when not seen in that nearly nonexistent light. Holmes grabbed one of the lanterns and swung it over the body. The shadows shifted crazily across the room, and for a minute I nearly felt myself dizzied by them, as the sudden shift made me reach out to grab the table, unsure of where I stood.

Holmes was leaning over the face of the corpse, shifting this way and that, looking directly at it from the front, then up from under the chin, or at either side into the ears. Moving closer myself, I saw that the fellow was incredibly well preserved, considering how long he had supposedly been buried. His hair, what there was left of it, seemed rather long in the old style, and lay in wet, dark, and lanky locks across his brow. His chin was firm, although his mouth sagged open, and his lips had receded, exposing teeth in rather bad condition. His nose had caved in, as would be expected, and of course his eyes, which were closed, were sunken.

"What would you estimate this man's age to have been at the time of his death, Watson?" Holmes asked.

I considered my answer for a moment. "As I'm sure you are aware," I finally answered, "there are a number of factors to take into account. However, my best conclusion at first glance would be that he was in his early twenties."

"I concur," said Holmes.

"Then this cannot be the body of Martin Briley's father, who died in 1840."

"Correct."

"Mr. Briley's father, Galton Briley, is buried in the family mausoleum," said Burton.

Holmes did not respond. Taking a blunt metal probe from his pocket, about five inches long, he attempted to push open one of the closed eyelids. Initially it refused to move, but then the upper lid slowly parted from the lower, revealing an empty cavity within.

"Mr. Holmes!" said MacDonald, his experience as a policeman clearly overcome by the instinctive revulsion against the death that all of us carry within us at some level.

"It was too much to hope for," said Holmes, pulling the probe away from the dead man's eye. "I wished to see if any of the eye remained. I had hoped to determine what color his eyes had been. It might have given us a clue as to his family relations."

"Yes, yes, indeed," said MacDonald, clearly embarrassed at slightly losing his professional composure. "I understand."

Holmes moved the lantern as he stepped along the table, examining the fellow from head to foot. He paid particular attention to the shoes of the dead man, before finally returning to the fellow's right hand, which I had wanted him to examine all along.

Gingerly picking up the hand, as if it might fall apart, he held it close to the lantern's light. After a moment, he said softly, "Watson? Your opinion, please."

I stepped around the table and leaned down to where he was directing. Ignoring my own revulsion, I took the hand, finding it much firmer than I would have imagined. I had assumed it would be like those that have been in traditional graves for any amount of time. These soften and liquefy as the decay process proceeds. On the other hand, drowning victims' flesh often transforms through the process of saponification into a soap-like material, as can also happen in the presence of some type of alkali that mixes with the fats and oils of the body. Perhaps the fact that this corpse had been preserved in an acidic element explained why the flesh was solid, even after all these years.

I had heard something of the bog mummies, as they are called, who have been pulled from peat in many locations across Europe and northern Britain over the years. Some of these had been incredibly well preserved, even after centuries, and occasionally the very expressions on their faces are still intact. The body that we were examining that night in the rain-soaked cottage was perhaps the most well-preserved of any that I had ever heard discussed. No doubt, that had something to do with the fact that it had only been buried for a period of fifty years or so.

Careful examination of the side of the hand, with its thumb and only three fingers, confirmed what Holmes had wanted me to see. There was no sign of a scar whatsoever where the little finger was missing. I was able to feel the internal bones adequately through the well-preserved skin enough to make a determination.

"Dissection is the only way to confirm for sure," I stated, "but my preliminary examination seems to suggest that the missing finger was not lost due to some misfortune, and that the man was born this way."

"Thank you, Watson," said Holmes. Straightening up, he turned to MacDonald. "Has he been examined underneath his clothing?"

"No, sir. When I decided to ask for your assistance, I left the body as I found it. I can tell you that there are no tears in the clothing, and no sign of any wounds passing through the clothing, such as would come from the use of a knife or gun. I believe that Dr. Watson will be able to confirm the cause of death if he looks at the back of the fellow's head."

"Nevertheless," said Holmes, "I would like to examine the clothing and the rest of the body. Gentlemen, if you please?"

I could tell that for just one instant, MacDonald wanted to suggest waiting for the official autopsy. However, his faith in Holmes overwhelmed his internal objections, and he stepped closer to the table, in order to facilitate Holmes's request. MacDonald and I both undressed the corpse, with difficulty, one piece of clothing at a time. It was stained and fragile, but still remarkably intact. Holmes peered at the various items closely under the lantern light as they came off. It was hard to believe that it was still only early afternoon outside. It was as dark as night, adding to the unpleasant aspects of the experience.

Burton did not help scrutinize the body, but rather stood to the side a few feet, near the second lantern by the fireplace. I did not blame him at all. This macabre situation was obviously something new to him, and certainly nothing that he would care to repeat.

Holmes silently completed his appraisal of the clothing, and then started with the body itself, again moving from head to toe, before asking us to rotate the man over and onto his stomach, so that the reverse side could be investigated as well. I followed along at Holmes's side, seeing what he saw, and hopefully observing what he observed. Concluding his examination at the back of the man's head, Holmes pressed the scalp with his fingers for a moment before motioning me to take over. I quickly found that to which MacDonald had referred. There was a large concavity there, nearly the size of a cricket ball, under the remains of the man's dark-looking hair. There was no indication of any broken skin. The wound would have been fatal, although I cannot say if it would have resulted in an immediate death. I stated as much to Holmes, who nodded.

"Conclusions, gentlemen?" he said. "Watson?"

"In the absence of any other information at this time, such as evidence of poisoning, I would expect that the cause of death was due to the obvious blunt trauma to the back of the head, located in the occipital region. Other bones, including the neck, appear to be intact, although only an autopsy can confirm some of this for sure. He appears to have been a thin fellow in his early twenties. Although his teeth are in bad shape, they do not appear to be worn enough to indicate that he was any older than that. The same for the soles of his feet. He grew up wearing shoes that were too tight, but there are not any calluses that might be on the feet of an older man. Or a working man, for that matter. Also, his hands are smooth, as near as I can determine, showing that he was not involved in manual labor, at least for some time immediately before his death.

"MacDonald?" said Holmes.

"Well, other than the wound on his head, and the missing finger, I'm not sure what else there is to see."

"Come, MacDonald, do not be too timid. Did you not observe anything of interest about his clothing?"

"No, Mr. Holmes. It seems like regular clothing that one might have expected to encounter in the 1830's and '40's."

"True, true, but there is more. The clothing appears to be homemade, and sturdy enough for common labor. The shoes are also very tough, and as Watson pointed out, they appear to have been too tight. In fact — "

He stopped, and held up a shoe against the bottom of the corpse's foot, using his other hand to straighten it against the sole of the shoe. " — these shoes do not fit at all." The foot, in spite of being buried for a half-century, still extended nearly an inch past the length of the shoe.

"Perhaps I misjudged earlier, Holmes," I said. "I had concluded that he grew up wearing shoes that were too tight, but perhaps I was just seeing the effect of his feet being forced into the smaller shoes over the last fifty-odd years."

"No, you were correct in your statement, Watson. His toes are naturally contorted from growing up in tight shoes throughout his formative years. However, one only has to observe the length of his overall foot, compared with the sole length of the shoes, to see that these are too small for him, much smaller than what he would have worn simply to cramp his toes.

"Granted, some shrinkage has occurred to the corpse over time, but not as much as one might expect, as it was buried in the preserving medium of the acidic peat, and therefore did not completely mummify."

After we had all observed the point that Holmes was making, he gently lowered the leg back to the table. "Clearly, the foot is too long for the shoe, or to put it another way, the shoes are too small for the feet. Thus, these shoes did not belong to this man, and he was not buried in his own shoes. And to extrapolate from this conclusion, these were not his clothes either. This is confirmed by the fact that he does not appear to have done manual labor, as shown by his smooth hands and feet, while the clothes he is wearing *are* those of a laborer."

"So you think he was a gentleman, then?" interrupted Burton.

"It is quite possible," said Holmes.

"And he's missing a finger, like many of the Brileys. It wasn't cut off at some earlier date. You agree that he was born that way."

"That is true."

"Well, how could that be?" asked Burton. "I grew up here. I was taken in by Mr. Martin Briley as a boy, and I know all that there is to know about them. Mr. Briley never had any brothers or sisters. And he never had any cousins either. From 1840, when his father died, until now, he's been the last of the Brileys, and I believe that he will die that way."

"So you have no theory as to who this poor fellow might be?" asked Holmes.

"None in the world," replied Burton.

"Then we can expect nothing else from you about him then," said Holmes, rather abruptly. Thankfully, Burton did not seem to take offense.

Holmes walked to the foot of the table and grabbed the long fabric bundled there. As I lifted the lantern from the table, he hefted the sheet and started to pull it back over the body. Reaching the head, he began to lay it gently over the man's face before stopping himself. Pulling it back slightly, he leaned down and looked at the side of the man's head. "Watson, the lantern for a moment, if you please."

I edged it closer, trying to move it so that it wouldn't cast shadows from Holmes and his cap. He stared intently at the body's ear for a moment, and then stood and walked around to the other side. I followed and held the lantern while he repeated his actions. Then, having seen what he wanted to see, he stood and completed covering the now unclothed corpse.

"What did you notice, Mr. Holmes?" asked MacDonald.

"Hmm? Just a fact to document for later, Inspector. It may mean nothing, and then again, it may be a confirmation of sorts. And now," he said, gesturing toward the door, "let us return to the house, where we shall ask some questions, and possibly, I hope, find something hot to revive us."

"I can assure you of that, gentlemen," said Burton, leading us outside. We paused while MacDonald relocked the door, and then wound our way between the buildings until we found our waiting carriage, which had somehow made it back up the hillside. The rain seemed to have eased for a moment, but a cold wet wind was blowing, and the southwestern sky was filling with a new group of tall black clouds, spanning around to the north. As we moved past the lighted windows of the different cottages, I could see Holmes, looking at Burton with intense speculation, although Burton himself seemed completely oblivious to that fact.

As we were about to depart the collection of snug houses, Holmes suddenly reached out and grabbed Burton's shoulder. "Wait," he said. "Before we go back to the house, tell me where we can find the men who first discovered the body. Are they here, within these cottages?"

"I'm sure they're at the inn, back toward the village," replied Burton, signaling the carriage driver, who had started to slow, to move on. "You passed through it shortly before arriving at the house. I will send a message down that you wish to speak to them later, after we have warmed ourselves for a while at the house."

"That will be satisfactory," replied Holmes, settling back against the wet seat.

Holmes seemed to be satisfied with some secret knowledge, but I could not think of anything that we had seen so far that would provide any answers whatsoever. However, this was not an unusual situation for me, and I was content with the understanding that all would eventually be revealed. While I pondered Holmes's apparent confidence, he happened to glance up, catching my attention. Spotting the familiar gleam in his eye, I knew that he had caught the scent, and the game was once again afoot.

Chapter 4 – A Respite

There was no further conversation as we crossed the bridge over the stream, now even more noticeably swollen than when we had first passed this way, little more than an hour before. I foresaw that it would only continue to rise, as the rains from upstream collected and poured down in ever-increasing flows to join the channel. I began to ask Burton if the cottages were ever cut off from the rest of the estate by high water, but withheld the question, deciding that casual conversation while driving through the returning storm would be both unwise and unpleasant.

By the time we had reached the entrance to the house, the wind seemed to have shifted slightly, and held a cooler feel to it. I observed that Holmes seemed to be unaffected, as usual, but MacDonald and Burton had their hands thrust into their coat pockets, and the collars were pulled up around their necks, as was mine. Before we reached the door, it was thrown open by a man. He was small, not quite over five feet in height, but otherwise all was hidden as the warm welcome light from the hall spilled out behind him into the night-like darkness.

Stepping inside, we quickly divested ourselves of our outer attire, which the young man, as I could now see he was, gathered in his arms. Burton gave him quiet instructions about where to carry them in order to have them dried. I noticed that our traveling bags, both mine and Holmes's that had been carried in by MacDonald when we first arrived at the house, were lined up along the wall beneath an ornate mirror. Burton frowned. "I had planned to invite you gentlemen to stay with us here in the house for the night," he said. "I left instructions along those lines before I departed to meet you at the mere. I'm not sure why your bags haven't been taken upstairs."

"There is no need," began Holmes, but before he could continue, a voice interrupted from an archway at the back of the hall.

"I gave the instructions to keep the bags down here, Mr. Burton," said a woman, entering with a firm and purposeful step.

"Indeed, Mrs. Lynch. And by what authority did you go against my wishes?"

She stopped about ten feet in front of us. She was tall, well over five-and-a-half feet. Her height was accentuated by the way in which her hair was pulled up into what can only be described as a crown on her head. It was an iron grey, with streaks of white interestingly woven throughout. There were no loose strands whatsoever, and her ears were completely exposed. She had a rather thin nose, and her mouth was a wide tight line, her lips pursed in irritation. Her hands were clasped loosely at waist level, in something of a prayerful repose, although there was nothing holy about her expression.

She wore no jewelry whatsoever, and her dress was black, in a style I had not seen in more than a decade. Her entire figure presented itself as that of a harsh schoolmistress, who was highly displeased with a rebellious student — in this case, Burton.

This displeasure found its expression and focus through her eyes, which were barely visible as she looked out beneath lowered lids. She took another step forward, changing the angle of the light when it hit her face as she looked at Burton, who was just slightly taller than she. I could suddenly see her face was lined with a fine mesh of countless lines and wrinkles that had not been visible just a moment before. Clearly, she was at least twenty years older than her early fifties, the age at which I had first placed her.

"The master has given you authority over the running of the estate, Mr. Burton," she said. "It does not extend to the household."

Burton did not back down in the least. When we had first entered the well-lit hallway, I had seen Burton clearly for the first time. As he had removed his rain apparel and stood in the light, I had concluded that he looked to be a friendly but capable individual, who naturally radiated the competence and leadership that would be required for his position as an estate agent. Now, when challenged by Mrs. Lynch, he retained his authority, but his good-natured manner disappeared.

"We will offer these men, who have come here to help us, the hospitality of the estate, Mrs. Lynch. The *entire* estate. The authority vested to me does not stop at the front door of this house, no matter how much you would like to wish it so."

"I do not believe the master would wish us to provide lodging for *policemen*," she sniffed.

"And I believe that you and I will go to the master and discuss it with him." He turned to us, clearly embarrassed, yet in control of the situation. "Gentlemen, if you will wait in this room?" He gestured through an open double door on the left side of the hall. "I understand Inspector MacDonald was in that room yesterday. In the meantime, Mrs. Lynch and I shall speak to Mr. Briley."

He turned back to her, and with a stiff wave of his arm, offered to let her go first toward some other part of the house. She stood without speaking for a moment, and then, without any physical signs of surrender, spoke in the same tone as before, saying, "There will be no need to discuss this with the master at the present time, Mr. Burton. However, you can be sure I will be approaching him in the very near future to make sure there is a clear understanding of where the responsibilities of the estate start and where they end."

"I look forward to it," replied Burton. "And now, will you see about preparing rooms for these gentlemen? Also, we require food and drink. *Warm* food, if you please."

He turned toward us, gesturing again toward the room, clearly dismissing the older woman. "Gentlemen? If you wouldn't mind, we can go in and find seats by the fire."

He followed us in, and turned and shut both doors. Then, turning to face us, he visibly and almost comically relaxed, before letting a small grin cross his face.

"Whew," he said, "St. George versus the Dragon." He moved to a table holding a bottle containing what looked like brandy and some glasses. "I think we're safe in here now. For the moment, at least."

He opened the bottle, grabbed the first of the glasses, and started to pour. "Drinks, gentlemen? Mr. Holmes? Doctor? Inspector?"

With the tension released, I felt a smile come to my face, as MacDonald replied, "Well, I am on duty, I suppose, but I don't think anyone would mind if I had a restorative on a day like this."

"Here, here," I concurred, stepping forward to receive the second glass poured, after that given to MacDonald. "I can attest to the healing powers of brandy for these conditions."

Holmes remained silent while accepting his glass. Burton finished by pouring one for himself, and then raised it. "To the conqueror and his brave companions." He tipped up the glass, said softly, "Until next time," and turned to refill it.

MacDonald did not wait to be asked as he stuck out his glass as well. Holmes still held his, only one sip taken, while I considered my glass and decided not to have more on a quite empty stomach.

"There seems to be," Holmes began, "some tension in the house. I'm sure that I speak for Watson and MacDonald when I state that we do not wish to cause you any difficulties. We had always intended to stay at the inn in the village, should our investigation take longer than a day."

"Indeed," I added. "We don't want to force you to fight a battle before you need to."

"Do not worry, doctor. Disagreements with Mrs. Lynch occur one way or another on a nearly daily basis. I am quite comfortable with my understanding of my position on the estate, and where my limits are set."

"So you have the complete confidence of Mr. Briley, then?" asked Holmes, rather impolitely, to my mind.

"I believe that I do," said Burton, gesturing us toward the fire. We adjusted our seats so that each had access to the drying warmth, and then Burton continued. "I have been trained by Mr. Briley for this position, having been hand-picked, as it were, when I was just a lad, and I was long ago given to understand that my authority, when needed, also extended over Mrs. Lynch. As you said, doctor, I do pick my battles with her, but occasionally there *is* a battle that needs to be fought. She keeps an excellent household, there is no doubt about that, even if it is run too strictly for my taste. I certainly have no wish to interfere with the day-to-day workings of the place. In any case, I have my time well taken by the many tasks that call from outside the doors of the house."

"You say that you were hand-picked," said Holmes. "How exactly did that occur?"

Burton did not answer immediately, but instead, went and recharged his glass. He raised it with questioning eyes in our direction. Holmes and I shook our heads. MacDonald looked as if he dearly would like a third glass, but then reluctantly declined. Burton added a slight amount to his glass, and then returned to his seat.

"I was born and raised in the village, Mr. Holmes," he said. "It is a small place, and does not even really have a name, as it is not so much a village as a wide spot in the road on the way to Mr. Briley's estate."

Burton shifted and took another sip. "Mr. Briley owns the land and the buildings, the same as he does where the cottages are located. The village is made up of a number of houses and shops, used by the estate workers. There is an inn with a pub in the ground floor, where the men of the estate gather to socialize.

"The road which you traveled from the station at Leighton is generally only used by people who have estate business. It goes on through to Woburn, to the northwest, but as there is a more direct route, we rarely have any strangers passing through.

"As I said, I was born in the village. My father died before I was born, and my mother raised me alone and worked as a seamstress. Actually, she was the primary seamstress for the village. When quality work was needed, it was to my mother that the villagers turned.

"When I was ten years of age, in 1864, she caught a sudden illness, and within a few days, she was gone. Up until that time, I had given no thought to my future. I had worked as needed around our home, and had gone to school as was expected. We have always had an excellent school here, one of the finest around, started and financed by Mr. Briley."

"I have heard of it," said Holmes. "It is a model of how an estate owner who is willing to spend a little extra can reap much greater rewards for his efforts. I believe he started it when he was a young man, soon after he inherited the estate."

"That is correct, Mr. Holmes. It was revolutionary at the time. There was certainly nothing else like it in England for many years. I understand he was initially heavily criticized, but the subsequent results more than silenced his detractors. And in any case, it was his land and his money, and he apparently did not care what anyone thought of him."

"And you were attending the school at the time of your mother's death?" I asked. "Were you even then being prepared for the running of the estate?"

"Not then, doctor," replied Burton. "In those days, I had no more than a vague awareness of Mr. Briley. There was some talk at the time of my mother's death that I would be accepted as an apprentice to one of the village craftsmen. That I might have become a blacksmith was a very strong possibility. But before a decision was made, Mr. Briley himself came to the neighbor's house where I had been staying since my mother's death.

"I had seen him before then, of course. He was not a large or imposing man, even in those days before age caught up with him, and there was certainly nothing frightening about him, in spite of his authority. But whenever he rode through town, people stopped and indicated their respect to him, doffing their caps or touching their foreheads. There was no irony to it, gentlemen. Mr. Briley has done a lot for this village, and there isn't anyone here who has not been touched in some way by his generosity or benevolence toward the community.

"The day Mr. Briley came to get me, I heard a horse stopping in the yard. Like the other children in that house, I ran to the windows and then to the door to see who it was.

"He was wearing a long cloak, and, it being a cold day, his face was bundled and hidden. Yet we knew who he was, if only from the fine strapping horse he was riding. He rode often in those days, and they said he had ridden even more in years past, before age started to overtake him.

"He was in his mid-forties then, and still a very vital and active manager of the estate. His gaze was always solemn, but his eyes could express amusement or approval, even as they could darken when he was displeased.

"He politely asked permission to enter, and of course it was given. He spoke for a moment or two to the owners of the house, in low tones. All of the children, myself included, started to scatter to the back rooms, as was the custom when adults wanted to discuss adult business. But my name was called, and I was told to stay.

"Returning cautiously to the main room, I found Mr. Briley, who was then uncloaked, sitting on a stool by the fire. He held a mug of something in his hands. The good woman of the house prodded me forward, where I stood while Mr. Briley peered intently, first at my face, and then up and down quickly, before again meeting my eyes with his frank and appraising gaze.

" 'George,' he said, surprising me with his question, "are you an intelligent young man?'

"I was not able to speak at first, until I felt someone nudge me from behind. As he asked it again, no doubt fearing I was not intelligent at all, I managed to reply, 'I believe I have my fair share, sir,' I said, all in a rush, and perhaps a bit impertinently, now that I think on it.

"He didn't seem to think there was anything forward at all about my answer. He nodded gravely, and said he wanted to make a proposal. 'I'm aware of your unfortunate loss,' he said. 'I believe I have a place for you, if you would like it. It means hard work, and a willingness to learn. I hear good things from your teacher. I think you're the right man for the job.'

"I thanked him, not knowing at that age how to take being called a man. I stammered something about arrangements having already been made for me to apprentice to the village blacksmith. I must have said it with a little bit of resigned despair, because it made Mr. Briley's eyes glimmer with amusement for the first time that afternoon.

" 'You misunderstand me, George,' he interrupted. 'I want someone to learn how my estate works. If you come live with me, I'll show you. Someday, if you learn the lessons, if you learn my way of doing things, you'll be running the place.'

"As you can all imagine, it took me a few moments to get my mind settled about that. Of course, it would mean leaving the world I knew, but I was not wise enough at that time to realize that. The man and woman with whom I was staying started speaking over each other, complimenting Mr. Briley's generosity, while no doubt wondering why one of their own children was not picked.

"Whatever the reason, my belongings were gathered then and there, and I was put on the spare horse Mr. Briley had brought with him. There was no doubt that he had anticipated my acceptance of his offer. I rode with my new protector back to this house. Almost immediately my education began. Unfortunately, some of my practical lessons were learned thanks to Mrs. Lynch."

I expressed a sympathetic comment, and Burton nodded.

"Yes, you can imagine what that was like. She was the housekeeper even then, and from the first time I crossed the threshold here, she let me know that she disagreed with Mr. Briley's decision to bring me in as his ward. Oh, it was never a direct statement. It was simply sly comments here and there, often to the staff when Mr. Briley was not present, but where I couldn't help but to overhear. It might have gotten the better of me, and rather quickly, if Mr. Briley hadn't gone out of his way to make me feel welcome.

"He quickly showed me that he had been serious about teaching me the running of the estate. He made sure I had my lessons, as much as I could take in without foundering. But he also took me with him each day, to the fields and tenant farms, and to the buildings and shops that he owns in the village, pointing out to me different things I would need to know. He showed me how things work, and why. And most importantly, he gave me a better understanding that all of his employees here are people, and not just faceless laborers that can be replaced as one would a worn-out cog in a machine.

"By the time I was sixteen, I nearly had my growth, and the estate workers would listen to me as if I were the master himself. Mr. Briley had always made it clear that I spoke for him, and he would back what I said. When I was eighteen, I went away for some specialized learning, just for a year or so, and when I returned, I settled in as before, handling the day-to-day affairs.

"Throughout that time, of course, I have had my difficulties with Mrs. Lynch. She's been the housekeeper here since Mr. Briley's father was alive – she is in her seventies now, but doesn't look a day older than when I first came to live here. Sometimes Mr. Briley will defer to her in matters of the household or staff, but he has never let her criticisms of me stand whatsoever.

"In addition, she has often made free with her opinions about Mr. Briley's good works in the village and on the estate, criticizing what she often claims were unnecessary expenses just for the sake of charity. Mr. Briley lets her have her say. I suppose he's known her for so long that he must, but he never

48

lets what she says stop him from doing what he knows to be right."

At that moment, the doorway to the hall opened swiftly, as Mrs. Lynch herself stepped into the room. Her stance conveyed a hostile tension that led me to believe that she had been eavesdropping, and had heard Burton's frank statements concerning her. However, she intoned in an even voice, if unfriendly, "The food is ready, Mr. Burton. It's only shepherd's pie, which was to be for your dinner tonight, but it is no trouble to have it early for our *guests*."

Burton showed that he was aware of her ironic tone by flashing a suppressed grin to us. Standing, he gestured toward the hall. "I'm sorry, gentlemen, for running on so. However, I suppose it helped pass the time while we dried out before the fire until the food was prepared."

"Not at all, Mr. Burton," said MacDonald. "I myself rather enjoyed your tale. It's like something right out of a Dickens story."

Burton chuckled. "No doubt. However, I can assure you there is no person less like the old convict, Magwitch, than the good Mr. Briley." He seemed about to add something else, and then, with a smile, he stopped.

As we walked down the hall, Burton excused himself for a moment and spoke quietly to the young man who had let us in, and who was now loitering in a nearby doorway. Joining us, he explained, "I apologize, Mr. Holmes. I had forgotten I told you I would arrange to have the workmen who found the body meet us in the village. I've sent a message by Woods. The men should be at the inn a little later today in order to be questioned."

By this time, we were taking our seats in the nearby dining room. Mrs. Lynch stood off to the side, watching critically as a pretty maid offered cider to drink. I was surprised that a maid would be serving, but I decided that things were obviously run differently here in the Briley house. In the center of the table was a shepherd's pie. Obviously we were not going to stand on

49

ceremony, either because that was the custom of the house, or possibly because Mrs. Lynch was not going to provide any more hospitality than was required.

As we began to eat some of the excellent pie, Mrs. Lynch turned and silently left the room. The maid followed in her wake, and I happened to be looking up just as she glanced back and met Burton's eyes. His glance twinkled in her direction for just a moment, and I perceived the formation of a dimple on the girl's cheek before she vanished from the room. I surreptitiously looked toward Holmes and saw, unsurprisingly, that he had also observed the small communication between the two.

MacDonald was helping himself to the food with heart-warming enthusiasm. "Ver' good," he muttered, his Scots burr becoming stronger as the victuals warmed him from within.

Taking a sip of the cider, Holmes stated, "I would enjoy it if you would tell us some more about Mr. Briley's good works. I have heard a little of him in London, of course, but he is renowned for being something of a recluse, especially in these later years. For instance, there was some talk several years ago of his name appearing on the birthday list, but he somehow managed to have it removed, without offending Her Majesty."

"That's correct," said Burton, reaching for some more of the cider, centered on the table in a pitcher. "Would anyone care for more?" he asked. MacDonald accepted, while Holmes and I declined. "We make do for ourselves much of the time here. That includes serving ourselves at meals. Mr. Briley, now an invalid, eats alone and does not have social events requiring staff members trained for such events. In fact, he has never gone in for that sort of thing, even when he was up and about, and running the place himself."

"How long has he been incapacitated?" I asked, reaching for another helping of the pie.

"It has been about seven years since he first started to withdraw more noticeably from the running of the estate, several years after I returned and assumed more of the daily responsibilities. Up until then, he was quite visible, both here and in the village, although I was carrying out most of the daily management by then. He was able to spend more time with his local charitable works, and the school."

"Ah, yes. Tell us more of the school," said Holmes.

"Quite," said Burton. "Years before I was born, probably not long after he inherited the estate from his father, Mr. Briley set up the village school, which at that time was unlike anything anywhere else in Britain. He hired several teachers, instead of one master for all of the students, and he personally reviewed their methods on a regular basis in order to make sure they knew and understood their subjects, and also that they actually knew how to teach. Cruelty was never allowed. He made funds available for families so the children would not have to cease going to school in order to go to work to help provide for the family. He also established scholarships for promising village children, allowing many to continue into higher education. For those with less ability, he made certain they were well trained for jobs in the village or on the estate.

"Mr. Briley also hired a doctor soon after he came into his inheritance, paying the bills himself and making the man available to the whole village. In time, other doctors joined the first, and now there is a little hospital nearby, with free care for those who need it."

"Admirable," I said. "No wonder the man was offered a knighthood. Why did he refuse?"

"To be honest," responded Burton, "I've never really known. Mr. Briley's father had made a great deal of money when Mr. Briley was very young, and I've always had the impression that he did so in a rather ruthless manner. Sometimes, I've thought that Mr. Briley was trying to make up for his father's actions, which were fairly harsh, even for those rough days. On other occasions, I believe Mr. Briley had no wish to involve himself in the fripperies of the Court which might entangle him and take his time if he did accept a knighthood. He seemed to be more inclined to stay here, managing his properties and doing good works."

"And he never married?" I asked. "There was never a Mrs. Briley?"

"Never," replied Burton. "I understand that years ago, Mr. Briley had been living away from the estate in London for some time, and he only returned upon his father's death. I gather there was no good feeling between father and son in the later years of his father's life. As to what he did in the years when he was up in London, before his return, I have no knowledge. But I am certain he never married after he inherited the estate, nearly fifty years ago."

"And he had no brothers? No other family?" said MacDonald, wiping his mouth after pushing back his plate with a most satisfied sigh. He dropped the cloth with finality.

"No," said Burton, "at least none I've ever heard tell of. It has always been common knowledge in these parts that Mr. Briley was an only child, like his father before him."

"No heirs, eh?" said Holmes. I could tell that he wished to pull out his pipe, but was refraining. "Might I ask you a rather personal question?" Without waiting for a response, Holmes stated, "Are *you* his heir, Mr. Burton?"

Another man might have told Holmes to mind his own business, or to go to blazes, but Burton accepted the question with the open forthrightness that seemed to be his natural manner. "Honestly, Mr. Holmes, I do not know. There are many people who *believe* me to be the heir, and I *was* trained in order to run the place, but Mr. Briley has never once indicated to me one way or another who his heir is, or if he has even designated one. The estate is not entailed in any way, as it was all built on the funds obtained from the commerce of Mr. Briley's father, and to a degree that of his grandfather. Mr. Briley has been a careful steward, and has increased the assets of the estate many times over from the already vast amount he inherited from his father. I can tell you that because I have complete access to Mr. Briley's accounts, and his full confidence in carrying out the estate's business. But as to your question regarding an heir? As I said, I cannot tell you."

"I thank you for your willingness to answer my question. I cannot say whether or not it is of any relevance, but all knowledge is valuable, especially when trying to assemble a puzzle of this type."

I nearly snorted at this, as at times past Holmes has made some rather outrageous statements regarding the need to keep his brain-attic clear of unnecessary information. I believe that he knew what I was thinking in that moment, but he continued with this thought.

"Obviously, we have questions about Mr. Briley's family and heirs, as the body was found with the characteristic missing finger. Can you think of anyone you may have heard mentioned, or any name that you might have seen in a document, at any time, that could offer some clue as to who the dead man might have been?

"None, Mr. Holmes, none at all. And I assure you it has been weighing heavily on my mind since the body was found."

"I believe that Inspector MacDonald had a limited interview with Mr. Briley yesterday, but was unable to ascertain any specific facts relating to the investigation. Have you discussed it with him since then? Was he able to offer any theories? After all, the body has been here since the approximate time when he inherited the estate. I would think that the whole question would have some fascination for him."

"I have not spoken with him about the matter, gentlemen. Mr. Briley's health has been somewhat . . . fragile in the last year or so. When I saw how he reacted yesterday to the Inspector's questioning, I resolved not to pursue it on my own, unless it was first broached to me by Mr. Briley himself."

"He made it clear he did *not* want to talk to the likes of me," said MacDonald wryly.

"I understand, Mr. Burton," said Holmes. "However, I am very much afraid that we do not have the luxury of making that allowance again. I will also need to ask Mr. Briley some questions." Holmes pushed back his chair and stood, causing a small expression of surprise to widen Burton's eyes with the suddenness of the motion. "Is Mr. Briley available right now? I would like to begin questioning him as soon as possible."

A flat voice answered from the hall, growing louder as the speaker entered the room. "Mr. Briley is not available for visitors," said Mrs. Lynch. I wondered how long she had been standing in the hallway, lurking and listening. Surely we had not said anything objectionable?

"Mrs. Lynch," said the Inspector, also rising to his feet. "You cannot deny to us — "

"Mr. Burton will tell you that Mr. Briley always naps during the mid-afternoon, and cannot be disturbed now. Perhaps later, in a few hours, before dinner, you may have a few minutes of his time."

"I'm afraid I must concur, gentlemen. Mrs. Lynch is correct. Mr. Briley is almost certainly asleep right now, and will be for several more hours. As he ages, he tends to nap at regular intervals throughout the day. Although I am not certain of it, I believe he remains awake through parts of the night, reading, or sometimes just staring into the fire."

"He does, indeed, Mr. Burton," said Mrs. Lynch.

"If we are unable to see him now," Holmes said, "then so be it." He pulled his watch from his pocket and checked the time. "We shall proceed to the village and interview the laborers who found the body, assuming that they have assembled and made themselves available as requested. Will Mr. Briley be awake at five o'clock then, Mrs. Lynch?"

The thin line of her mouth became even thinner, as she said shortly, "He will."

Holmes did not say anything for a moment, as he stood at Mrs. Lynch's side, looking at her with a surprised interest that only I, who had known him for so many years, would recognize. He was docketing some fact, though I knew not what. Then, with a flash of satisfaction, he responded.

"Excellent. Then, gentlemen, I am afraid," said Holmes, moving toward the hall, "that I must request you to join me as we again throw ourselves to the mercy of the storm and make our way toward the village. As I recall, Mr. Burton, it is not a far walk?"

"Not far, but likely to be unpleasant on a day such as this. Shall I summon the carriage?"

"Let us take a vote. Inspector?"

MacDonald did not want to appear any less able than Holmes to face unpleasantness. "I can walk it," he said. Turning to me, he asked, "Doctor?"

Apparently I didn't want to appear any less able than Holmes, either. "Let us get it over with," I said, already dreading it.

"Excellent, then," said Holmes. "To our coats, and then a quick march to the . . . south, I should think!"

Chapter 5 – At The Inn

The less said of that trek to the village, the better. During that time of my life, in the spring of 1888, I was fairly well healed from the wounds that I had received at the Battle of Maiwand. Keeping up with Holmes during his investigations over the years had been the best therapy I could ask for. He was always aware of my limits, and he never asked of me any more than I was capable of providing. Still, I occasionally felt the twinges of my Afghan wound, especially on days such as that. Without seeing it, I knew the glass was falling, and the ill weather only promised to worsen as the day progressed.

After a trek that descended almost imperceptibly toward the village, we found ourselves turning a corner and suddenly facing the inn door. The entrance was well lit, and the sign hanging over the door, boldly proclaiming "The Ram and Lamb", was striking in its color and clarity. Burton saw me notice it, and said, as we were stepping through the door, "You'll find all the shops and businesses in the village are well kept, doctor. It's just another example of Mr. Briley's excellent stewardship."

"And yours, surely, at this point," I replied as MacDonald closed the door behind us.

We began to shed our coats, and Burton replied modestly, "I'm just carrying out Mr. Briley's wishes. He laid out the pattern years ago, and I simply make certain that nothing changes."

Hanging our coats and hats on handy pegs by the door, we turned to face the room. It was not large by any means, perhaps twenty feet deep, with stairs on the left wall, and a pair of doors in the back, one standing open to reveal another room, much like this one, filled with tables, and also well-lit by lanterns. It was certainly cleaner than most of the other rooms of this type that I had previously encountered. Down the right side of the room in which we stood was the bar, with an unexpectedly large selection of various bottles behind it, presenting many different and enticing colors and shapes.

There were nearly a dozen or so men in the place, most sitting at tables, but a couple of them leaned against the bar. One had his back to it, elbows propped there like someone from the American Wild West. A serving girl moved among the tables. Behind the bar was a large, chipper fellow sporting a trimmed military moustache very similar to my own. He was holding a cloth and talking to the man who was facing him.

Conversation softened as we entered, and everyone stopped to glance in our direction. Upon recognizing our companion, Mr. Burton, the men seemed to relax, and they returned to whatever their previous business had been. The hum of their voices rose to the original volume, and the warm sound of glasses being raised and replaced on tables resumed. A few of the men threw friendly hands up in our direction. Burton responded with a matching gesture.

As we waited for a moment, huddled near the door and already enjoying the warmth from the blaze in the fireplace across the room between the two doors, Burton stepped to one of the tables where three men sat. He spoke to them for a moment, gesturing our way, and then looking back over his shoulder at us when the other men did so as well.

While they spoke, I took a moment to look around the bar. It was extremely well kept for such a place, in as good a condition as any that I've seen in my travels. And the patrons appeared to be healthy and happy.

My attention was drawn to one old fellow, sitting at a table near the fireplace. His back was to the flames, which were doing a good job indeed of heating the room. I imagined the man would be very warm in the seat that he had chosen. He was slumped, with a hand resting on the table before him, near an empty glass. The flickering firelight behind him added a strange cast to his snow-white hair.

"He's seventy-five if he's a day," said Holmes softly. Knowing him as I did, I was not surprised that he had observed where I was looking.

"He's certainly earned a rest," I said. "He appears to be enjoying a well-deserved slumber."

"Oh, he's not asleep," said Holmes. "He's been watching us through lowered lids since we arrived. Ah, there! You see?"

While Holmes had been speaking, the serving girl had brought a refill to the old man. She set it on the table and removed his empty glass. Without changing his posture or the expression on his face whatsoever, which I had believed to be the typical nap of the elderly, he reached his hand toward the fresh beverage and brought it steadily to his lips.

Burton finished speaking with the men at the table and stepped back. The men stood, gathering their glasses, and Burton turned and walked a few steps to the right of the room, speaking now in a low voice to the bartender. The man nodded in a friendly way, and gestured with a glance toward the back room. Burton then motioned us forward, and we joined the group, all making our way out of the main room.

Burton waited until we had all passed him, and then followed us. This room also had a cheery fireplace, set immediately behind the one in the main room. There were several tables, one large enough to have a place for all of us. Burton asked what we would have to drink. MacDonald ordered whiskey, Holmes and I brandy, while the three men wanted refills of beer. Burton left for just a moment to give the order to the tapster, and then returned, pulling the door behind him.

"While we wait, Mr. Burton," said Holmes, "would you mind introducing us?"

I knew that Holmes had no shyness about introducing himself, and he wanted the act to come from Burton, in order to have legitimacy and authority before these men. Burton then explained that both Holmes and I were criminal specialists down from London. I started to demur, but then decided not to confuse the issue.

Burton then introduced the large fellow in the middle, obviously regarded as the leader of the bunch, as Lambrick, while the older man to his right was Creed, and the fellow in his twenties on his left was Huggins.

Burton was explaining that the men had already been interviewed by MacDonald the previous day when the door reopened, and the man from the bar brought in our drinks. After distributing them, the fellow left, and Holmes began to speak.

"I'm aware that you were asked about finding the body in the trench yesterday by the Inspector. However, I beg of you to indulge me and repeat your story, trying to remember to tell it as fresh a manner as possible. Try not to think of it as you've previously repeated it, both to the authorities and to your friends, your family, and to the men out in the bar. I need you to see it as if it is new, so I may experience it through your eyes as if I were there."

The three men looked at one another, and then both seemed to defer to Lambrick, the large fellow in the middle. "Mr. Holmes, it was just another day. We had been working on digging that trench for nearly three weeks. I suppose you could say I was the foreman of the job, at least on times when Mr. Burton wasn't there. And you know we do a good job when you have to be away. Isn't that right, Mr. Burton?"

"Certainly. I have complete confidence in you," replied Burton.

"Tell me about that day," said Holmes. "What were the conditions? What time did you discover the body?"

"It was a sunny day, not too hot. It had rained some the day before, but not like what we're seeing today, and the ground wasn't too damp. It wasn't too long after our noontime meal," said Lambrick. "We had been pulling what was left of the tree out of the way in the morning, and then we kept digging to expose the pipe. We haven't always been digging down all the way to the old pipe, you understand. The old one was deep enough already that we had room to lay the new one near it, or on top of it, and still get a good fall so the flow would still go downhill."

"And why were you forced to dig deeper in this area?" asked Holmes.

"Well, we were at a point where the trench had turned less steep at the bottom of the hill and was starting to flatten out more as it neared the mere. Of course, we didn't want to go too deep, or we'd get into the groundwater. And then there was the tree. We had to dig down at that spot to make sure we got rid of the roots around there. Then we had to cut them back enough so they wouldn't interfere with the work."

"I see. And then you found the body. How did that occur?"

"It was Huggins what first saw it. He was digging on one side of the pipe and some of the dirt slid down, a big chunk, sudden-like, showing cloth. You tell him, Huggins."

The young fellow looked over at us, and then back at Lambrick. He took a long pull at his beer, wiped his sleeve across his mouth, stifled a belch, and said suddenly, "I swear to God I still wonder what'd happen if I'd've swung the pick right into him. I can almost feel it, d----d if I can't! Bloody nightmare stuff, by God!"

His sudden outburst caught us by surprise. I nearly laughed, and I could see the same expression in Holmes's face. MacDonald, on the other hand, scowled, and Burton looked mortified.

Lambrick glared at Huggins, and was about rebuke him, when Creed spoke, in a surprisingly even and educated voice.

"I believe, gentlemen," he said, "that I can answer your questions as well as my friends here. Incidentally, Mr. Holmes, perhaps you remember me? We met several years ago, when I was living out in Harrow Weald, where my people come from. You came to my place of employment, to ask us all some questions."

I saw Holmes's face flicker with recognition. "Ah, yes. Mr. Jeremiah Creed, the school teacher. And how is your brother? Still practicing law?"

Creed's expression saddened. "Unfortunately, Mr. Holmes, he perished in a fire the year after your visit. He was rescuing a child trapped in one of the rooms above 'The Red Boar,' where you and Dr. Watson had met with us on that dark afternoon."

I remembered the fellow now, although I'm not surprised that I didn't identify him at first. He had changed much since the early spring of 1883, when Holmes and I had become involved in a large, complex case that tested all our skills and had permanently cemented our friendship. I had made notes of the matter at the time, as best I could, but the convoluted path of the investigation had been almost more than I could follow, even after Holmes's lengthy explanations.

Mr. Creed had certainly changed in the five years since I had last seen him. I wanted to ask how he had made the unlikely journey from school teacher to laborer, digging trenches to lay pipes carrying away the waste from worker's cottages. As I recalled, he had given a very clear account of the tall landlady's actions, back in 1883, during the Affair of the Seven Silver Clocks. It will be recalled that Holmes, by postulating the existence of the *eighth* clock, was able to show to Inspector Gregson that the man from Trinity College had left the room *before* the explosion of the dynamite bomb, when he shouldn't have known to leave at all.

Creed took a sip of his beer, but unlike Huggins, he did not burst forth emotionally. Rather, he calmly explained that the collapse of dirt around the pipe had revealed the corpse's leg. "The left leg," he said, specifically. He went on to make clear that the body was lying in the direction of the pipe, rather than perpendicular to it, and completely under it as well. The head was resting toward the uphill side, and the feet in the direction of the mere.

"And after the body was first exposed, what did you all do?" asked Holmes. "Was there anyone else in the immediate vicinity, other than you three?"

"No, sir," said Creed. "When we first started digging, a few weeks ago, some of the village boys would hang around, curious about what we were doing. For that matter, so would some of the villagers and people who lived in the cottages, who would walk down when they had a free moment. But as the weeks progressed, the sight of digging down and connecting up yet another segment of pipe became boring for them. There was no one else there when we found the body."

"And Mr. Lambrick, was it you who summoned the authorities?"

"Yes, sir, it was. After we dug it out some more, I went to find Mr. Burton here. I didn't send Huggins because, well, he was right upset about the whole business, and also I didn't want him telling everyone he saw along the way, and leading back a hundred people as if they were going to look at the circus."

"After Mr. Burton arrived, did you resume removal of the body?"

"Well, Creed and Huggins did, under Mr. Burton's direction. I went to find the Constable and the Doctor. I was to make sure I didn't tell anyone what had been discovered, and also to see that no one saw me bringing them back, so that questions wouldn't be asked."

"And when you returned, was the body completely uncovered yet?"

"Not all the way, sir. It took at least another hour, because we had to scrape away around and under it, so that we didn't cause it any damage. It turned out to be sturdier than we first imagined."

"How long did it take you to get back with the other two men?"

"Not long at all," replied Lambrick. "When we got there, Mr. Burton explained the situation to them, and said he hoped to avoid a lot of gossip until we knew exactly what we had uncovered."

Holmes was silent for a moment, and then turned slightly, asking, "Mr. Creed, was there anything underneath the body or in the surrounding soil that might have provided a clue?"

Creed looked at Holmes frankly. "No, sir. We did look, of course, after the body was removed. After we dug some on its left side, I moved around to the other side and dug down there, so I was able to loosen it."

"On the body's right side?" said Holmes.

"Yes, sir. I wanted to loosen up the soil there, so when we pushed him toward his left, and the larger hole near where the tree had been, it would be easier to get him out. When it was finally time to remove the fellow, we carefully slid a tarp under him from the original hole, on his left side, and I pulled it up on the right. Then it was passed back through over the top of him, rubbing against the bottom side of the pipe, and the whole thing was pulled out that way. Then we finished wrapping him up, loaded him on the carriage, and the doctor took him back up to the cottages with Mr. Lambrick, who helped carry the body into an empty house there."

"That's right, sir," agreed Lambrick, attempting to look helpful as he glanced frequently toward Burton.

Huggins continued to contemplate the last half-inch of beer in his glass, and once, with a shudder, he muttered an unattached "By God!" to himself.

"Did you all comment on how well the body was preserved?" asked Holmes.

Lambrick nodded. "Yes, sir, we did. Mind you, we only saw his face and one of his hands, but they were tanned, like leather. Mr. Burton told us it was from soaking up the groundwater so near the mere. The earth there is almost like peat, and I've heard tell of other people found that way, up north. Mr. Burton said it's something that's in the water. It's tan . . . tan . . . . "

"Tannin," said Burton. "It's what makes the leaves turn brown in the fall. After the green colors fade away."

Lambrick nodded, and Holmes said, "Thank you, Mr. Burton." He had been leaning forward, his gaze taking in all three of the men in that hawk-like way. Lambrick, solid and middle-aged, had faced him with an open gaze, simply answering the questions as asked. Creed had sat forward, alert and watchful, his pose mimicking that of Holmes, although on a much smaller scale. And Huggins, almost still a boy, had attended at times, but on other occasions seemed to be lost in his own thoughts.

Holmes sat up straighter, indicating that the interview was at a close. "I thank you, gentlemen, for your time. I appreciate your willingness to meet here and discuss this matter, especially on a day such as this." He looked toward MacDonald. "Do you have any further questions, Inspector?"

"No, Mr. Holmes. I spoke to these men yesterday, and their stories match what I heard then."

"Watson?" asked Holmes.

I simply shook my head. Holmes then stood, and we all followed. "Then, again, I thank you all."

"Not at all, sir. Just doing our duty," said Lambrick, with a nod toward Burton, who returned it. Then the three men moved toward the door. Creed reached it first, opened it, and stepped aside, allowing Burton, the older man, and the younger to precede him. As he started to follow, Holmes said, "Oh, Mr. Creed. Just another word, if you don't mind?"

Creed turned around, and did not seem surprised. He started to shut the door, but Holmes stopped him. "No need for that," he said. "Doctor Watson and the Inspector will wait for us in the other room."

Seeing as how we had been suddenly dismissed, MacDonald shared a look with me, where his amusement was revealed only by the smile in his eyes, and we walked out of the room. I started to close the door, but Holmes said, "Leave it, Watson. We will only be a moment."

MacDonald and I went out into the larger room. The conversation did not stop, but there was a perceptible decrease in volume. MacDonald went to the bar to order a wee dram, as he put it. I was sorely tempted to join him, as the pain in my leg continued to increase, even as the barometer was no doubt falling. In spite of the intensity of the storm we had we witnessed throughout the day, I had no doubt that things were going to get worse as night came on.

Burton stood at the side of the room, talking to Lambrick and Huggins. Several of the other men in the room cast their eyes toward them, but made no move to join the conversation. I watched the old man near the fireplace. He still looked as if he were collapsed in sleep, but now that I had been made aware of the situation, I could see he was watching everything very closely indeed through lowered lids.

Holmes and Creed walked back through the door. They stopped just this side of it, and Holmes offered his hand. "Again, Mr. Creed, I'm sorry to hear about the loss of your brother. He was a good man, and of great assistance to us."

"Thank you, Mr. Holmes," said Creed. "Your thoughts are much appreciated." Creed then joined Lambrick and Huggins, while Burton broke away to rejoin our party.

"Did you find out anything else from Creed, Mr. Holmes?" said MacDonald, softly so that none of the other men in the room could hear.

"I was simply expressing my condolences to Mr. Creed for the loss of his brother four years ago," Holmes replied, in an equally quiet tone.

"And I'm just going to grow wings and fly back to Briley House," whispered MacDonald, but with a good-natured smile. "Is it a secret, then?"

"Not at all," replied Holmes. "I just wanted to confirm that I had received the message that Mr. Creed was sending."

"Message?" murmured Burton. "What message?"

"That he *did* recognize that the body found showed the distinctive characteristic of the missing Briley finger. He was at great pains several times to point out that the left side of the body, with its whole hand, was first exposed, that *he* was the man on the right side who dug down and uncovered that segment, and that when the tarp was passed through and back, the right side was then covered before Lambrick or Huggins had a chance to see the malformed hand.

"Although he does know about the hand, and he recognizes the significance of it, I am certain he will not reveal anything to anyone here, or elsewhere, for that matter."

"And why not?" asked MacDonald. "Information like that would get drinks for someone all night long, at the very least."

"You forget that Watson and I have encountered Creed before, Inspector. While we only knew him for a short time, and certainly his circumstances have come down in the world since then, I believe him to be a man of better character than that. Also, he simply has an appreciation for knowledge, and is happy knowing something of the truth, without having a compulsion to reveal it.

"He told me that when the very first segment of the body was revealed, he recognized it as an old corpse. He understood the nature of peat mummification, and realized that perhaps he was seeing something along those lines. Then he perceived from design of the clothing, and also the location of the body right underneath the pipe, that it was *not* one of the peat mummies such as those found in the northern climes, and that this body was more modern than that, though not recently buried. It was no great leap to decide that if a body was hidden in that way, it was probably related to a murder. Only when he saw the right hand did he realize the family connections that were implied."

MacDonald glanced over at Creed, who happened to be looking our way. Creed gave a nod, which MacDonald returned. The tall Inspector, who had still been holding his now-empty wee glass, set it on the bar and asked, "Well, Mr. Holmes, to whom can I guide you next?"

66

Holmes pulled out his watch. "I believe it's still more than an hour until Mr. Briley will be awake. Is that correct, Mr. Burton?"

Burton leaned over to see Holmes's watch, which Holmes turned to provide a better view. "That's right, Mr. Holmes. Although I would allow a little extra. He generally awakens at about the same time, but then he has tea with a little something before his dinner is brought in, a few hours later."

Holmes nodded. "Then I propose to spend some more time here, getting to know a few more of the locals. Watson, do you care to join me?"

I shook my head. I had been considering for a few minutes now that it would serve me well to get back to the house and get off my aching leg. I held up my cane and indicated that I would be returning with the others.

"Actually, doctor," said MacDonald, "if Mr. Holmes doesn't need anything from me right now, I have to arrange to have the body moved into Woburn for the autopsy."

"And I need to be checking on the cottages," said Burton. "If the rains continue, as it seems they will, they might be cut off by the stream later tonight, as has happened before and will happen again. They are only a few hundred yards from the main house, but it might as well be out on Lizard's Point at high tide when that stream gets up. I need to make sure that everyone will be all right if they can't get out for a day or so. One of the women is expecting, for instance, and it might be a good idea to move her up here to the village for the duration."

Holmes nodded, and rubbed his hands together. "So be it. I will plan on meeting you all back at the house at half past five. Barkeep! A glass of your beer." And with that, he turned away from us and stepped up to the counter, beginning an animated conversation with the ruddy man who placed a glass in front of him.

With an understanding smile shared between us all, we remaining three returned to the storm. We walked back up the grade toward the house, and luckily the wet wind was behind us. Had I realized when we made our way down to the village that the reverse journey would require much more effort, as it was all uphill, I might have voted to have the carriage hauled out after all. When we finally reached the house, Burton offered to go in with me, but I waved him off. He and MacDonald then turned and continued around the house toward the cottages and their various tasks. I did not envy them at all.

Chapter 6 – An Overheard Conversation

I tried the knob of the great door, and found it to be unlocked. Stepping into the large entry hall of the main house, I then pushed the door shut behind me to find a silence that seemed almost other-worldly after the tumult outside. I was shedding my wet coat and hat when the lad who had greeted us earlier rushed up and took my things, apologizing that he had not known I was there. I relieved him of any responsibility, and asked if it would be possible to get a hot drink, preferably with something tipped into it. He assured me that he would be back very shortly with what I requested, and — with a not-so-subtle glance at the water puddled inside the front door, marking the site of my entrance, he walked off into another part of the house, while I stepped into the sitting room where we had tarried earlier, before being called in for our late lunch.

I settled into a comfortable chair, after determining that my outer coat had kept my clothing dry enough so as not to damage the fine old piece of furniture, and pushed my feet toward the fire. It occurred to me that, just as I had heard how Briley had done so much for the village and the estate workers, he had also kept a very nice home for himself, even though he now got to see very little of it, staying in one room as he did, living as an invalid and to my knowledge refusing to venture elsewhere. The fire in this room had been going when we had arrived earlier, and it was still going even now. In some houses, it would have been tempting for the room to be closed off until needed, and doubtless it now often went unused. I did not have the impression that a great number of visitors made their way to Briley House.

While I was pondering these thoughts, the lad, whose name I recalled was Woods, brought me a tall — and of more importance — *hot* toddy. "I hope this will do the trick, sir," he said. With a sip, I nodded with satisfied agreement.

"Exactly what the doctor ordered," I said. He grinned, and asked if there would be anything else. I thanked him and said no, and he departed. I was glad that in a house run by such a martinet as Mrs. Lynch, there was still some happiness. Perhaps I was misjudging her. After all, the well-run house was a testimony to her management, and a woman who had been in charge as she had been for over fifty years was bound to get set in her ways. The reasons for her resentment against Burton were unclear, since he seemed a very capable and likeable individual, but it must be remembered that she had probably been running the house for over a quarter-century before he appeared on the scene, and doubtless she had disliked having her routine disturbed.

I shook my head and took a sip of the drink. It was useless to speculate on these matters. They had no bearing on the investigation, and I was sure that by tomorrow, Holmes and I would have returned to London. While the matter of the man with the missing finger, buried under the pipe and probably some relative of the Briley family, was certainly interesting, I did not know what Holmes's efforts could possibly reveal after so much time.

As I sat before the fire, with the sound of the rain lashing against the windows, I slowly fell again into the mood that had trailed me like a black dog throughout the early months of that year. I was nearly thirty-six years old, and what was I doing with myself? I had returned from Maiwand with my health irretrievably shattered, or so I had believed. Many were the times when I had questioned where I would have ended up if I had not been introduced to Holmes by Stamford, my old dresser, on that New Year's Day of 1881. I might have, when realizing that I could no longer afford London, moved myself to the country, where I could have set out my shingle and found a way to start using my skills once again. Or more likely, I would have remained in London, pitying my situation, spending more money than I had, and drinking more than I ought, until I ended up like so many other unfortunate veterans that found their way to that Great Cesspool that is London, never to escape.

But that New Year's Day, and specifically the short trip to the Criterion, and then on to the chemical lab at St. Bart's, had been a memorable day indeed, and it had certainly made great changes in my life. It was not the first link in my life by any means, but it was an important one, and a solid one. It had been the link to which the rest of my life was inextricably attached. It was a strong link upon which to forge the rest of the chain, and I didn't regret the chain that followed at all. And yet, why was I so unsettled these last months? It was not simply grief for my dear departed wife. I was questioning my future. Was this my purpose? To accompany Holmes on his quests, with no further thoughts toward the next direction that my own life was to take?

All in all, I was certain that, whatever doubts I might be having, the meeting with Holmes on that day had probably saved my life. Sharing rooms on my limited and dwindling finances had certainly rescued me from penury and disgrace. Being under his watchful eye had quickly helped to limit my consumption of alcohol, which I was relieved to discover had not become a vile and uncontrollable habit. And most important of all, joining in Holmes's cases had given my mind something to focus upon, while the simple act of physical participation in the investigations had been better therapy for my wounds than anything else that might have occurred to me by way of my medical training. All of the unexpected summonses from Holmes at whatever ungodly hours had never left me time to think *"I cannot do this."* I had simply been expected to rise from my comfortable fireside chair and assist my friend, and I had. Truly, I was in debt to him.

I took another sip of the excellent restorative as a log settled, and decided that I had no regrets about my time in Baker Street, and the events of my subsequent marriage. My time with Constance had been precious, if short. I had known that there was something terribly unfair about her illness, and how it kept us apart for great periods while she and her mother traveled and sought both relief and a cure. Even during those times, my friendship with Holmes had provided a distraction, as I often returned to Baker Street to assist him in his adventures. I'm afraid that my practice was neglected during this time, but in all honesty, my heart was simply not in building it up when Constance was not there to share it with me. And when she was gone, I had no interest in it at all. Once again, the old rooms at 221b were a refuge that I gladly sought.

So that early part of 1888 had been a time of questioning myself. I was nearing middle age. Was this all that I was supposed to be? I was an army veteran, no longer fit for army service. I was a doctor who had built and then let go of a practice. I was a widower. And I was the friend, assistant, advisor, and Boswell (at least in one short published narrative) of the man who was doing more to modernize the practices of criminal investigation than possibly anyone else in the world.

In spite of my doubts, and questions as to whether I should move on, reopen a practice, possibly find another wife with whom to share my life, I had to admit to myself that I actually enjoyed my involvement in Holmes's cases, in a way that I had never felt while in practice. It was akin to the rush that one felt when in combat, without the deadly boredom that comes in between skirmishes. Perhaps, I thought, this present sensation of being unsettled is how Holmes feels between cases, when his restlessness threatens to overcome him, and he likens himself to a machine, racing and tearing itself apart, because it is not fixed up properly to accomplish its intended work.

God help me, I realized that deep down I was even enjoying the matter that had called us out on that terrible day in Bedfordshire. I tried to imagine spending the same day at my old practice, seeing a dozen patients, each with the same symptoms as those of the day before. The rain would be sliding down the windows, and the hiss of the gaslight would go on and on, relentless in its efforts to lull me to sleep. And the next day would be a variation of the same. Was that really what I seemed to be wishing for? Of course, I terribly missed Constance, but even she had understood how I would anticipate a summons from Holmes, much like the reaction of a war horse when it hears the trumpets and senses the return to battle. She had understood it, and she had never begrudged it.

I drank the final sip of my drink, now cool on my tongue, and set the glass aside. I had reasoned my way through the black mood to the point where I was happy to be where I was, at least for now. The mood would return again throughout that spring, but with less and less power over me. And thankfully, Holmes and I would stay busy, pushing the problem further from my mind as the year passed.

But all of that was in the future. For now, I was simply grateful that I had recalled to myself that Holmes and I were doing important work. The warm drink and warmer fire had no doubt done their part to ease my troubled mind as well. I sank lower into the chair, considerably more at ease than when I had first placed myself there.

Some time later, a crack of thunder coincided with what could only be hail hitting the windows, and I pulled myself upright, surprised to find that I had fallen asleep. Looking at my watch, I saw I had been dozing for less than thirty minutes, and there was still a little time before we were to meet in order to speak with Mr. Briley in his chamber.

Standing and stretching before the fire, I looked to see that my empty glass was gone. Woods must have taken it while I slept. I did not want to return to my seat, and having nothing else to occupy me until my companions returned, I decided to explore the house.

Stepping out into the hallway, I glanced to my right, toward the heavy front door. I saw the water that had come in with me and had ended up on the floor was now gone. Woods had obviously removed more than my glass while I slept.

I walked to the other side of the hall and looked into an open door. This was another room, decorated very much like the one I had just departed. It too had a cheery fire going, but the room was darker. On the far side was another open door where much stronger light was showing. I crossed the darkened room and passed through into a smaller sitting room, with furniture of a style from several generations past, but in excellent condition. A mantle clock of great age made tired little whirring sounds as a counterpoint to the rain on the windows, and I realized that I had not heard any further thunder or hail.

The room seemed to be more of a museum piece than a place that was actually used on a daily basis. I was reminded of the similar room that Holmes and I had visited while confirming the last clue relating to the lost mine of the Duchy of Lancaster. We had been summoned to that lonely house by our friend, Alton Peake, the spiritualist. It was he, as might be remembered, who had called to Holmes's attention the footprints left by the supposed apparition, trailing to the forgotten priest's hole where the varnished palimpsest had been discovered. While I did not always agree with Peake's sincere belief in the supernatural, I must praise him for being rightly suspicious of so many of the charlatans that he exposed when they tried to pass off their mummery to a gullible public.

As I left that room, returning to the central hallway, but deeper into the house and across from the dining room where we had eaten earlier, I heard raised voices. Upon closer approach, they seemed to be coming from beyond the dining room. I passed in, and making my way around the large table, already set with four places for dinner later that evening, I stepped into a darkened hallway. It ran from the dining room into a butler's pantry. The door to the pantry was partly shut, but I could clearly hear the angry and clipped tones of Mrs. Lynch and George Burton.

"It is really none of your business at all," said Burton vehemently.

"It would not normally concern me," she replied, "except that the person in question is one of my maids, and I cannot — I *will not* — have anything like that going on my house!"

"Your house?" said Burton with incredulity. "I was under the impression that it was Mr. Briley's house. In each of the many ways he has taken me into his confidence, there has never been any mention in any of them that this was *your* house."

"I have run this house for longer than you can imagine, boy," said Mrs. Lynch with a menacing tone. "Nothing happens here without my knowledge or say so. Mr. Briley can do whatever he wants outside these walls. He can waste his money on that rabble in the village. He can build all the cottages he wants to shelter the workers. But what happens in this house is under *my* say-so. Mr. Briley understands that. He has understood it from the day he inherited it, and if you ask him, he will tell you so himself. You may have too much of your mother's blood in you to understand what you've seen in front of you from the day you got here, but I'm telling you as clearly as I can, this is *my* house, and if I intend to let a maid go for the good of running the place, I will!"

Burton was almost too angry to speak for a moment, and then he pulled himself in and replied in a very dangerous tone indeed. "You will never again speak of my mother, you evil crone. And as far as sending Lydia away, I can tell you it will do you no good at all. In fact, it will be a useful thing, in that my plans will simply be advanced. Lydia and I intend to marry, and if she is forced to leave, then we will simply marry all the sooner!"

"Marry! You would marry a *servant*, after you have been taken in by Mr. Briley and made his trusted ward? He won't stand for it. He would want you to marry someone of quality. Not a common — "

"Don't say it," said Burton. "Don't even say it, Mrs. Lynch, or I swear I'll have you out of here. You may have been here since you were a girl, and you seem to think that you will continue to stay here because you plan to live forever, but if you get in the way of my plans, I will see that you are put out of here immediately!"

75

"You wouldn't *dare!*" hissed Mrs. Lynch. "You don't even know what circumstances you're dealing with, boy. You should be grateful for the opportunity you have, and stop trying to rise above yourself before it is time."

"I can see that you fear what I've said, Mrs. Lynch. You know Mr. Briley will listen to me. Now I tell you, I could not care less if you continue to run this house the way you see fit until your last breath leaves your cruel body, no matter how much you seem to believe that will never happen. You do a good job here, and in spite of your sour disposition, the staff is actually content with you. I will put it to you simply: If you do not meddle in my affairs, then I will have no reason to conclude that you are my enemy, in spite of the way you have treated me since I came here as a boy. Now, I intend to marry Lydia, and if it needs to be sooner rather than later, so be it. So, tell me, Mrs. Lynch, Do we have an accord?"

From my hidden vantage point, I could not see either Burton or Mrs. Lynch, so I couldn't tell whether she nodded or rejected his question, but she gave no verbal indication either way to Burton's ultimatum. However, before any further conversation could continue, I heard the sound of the front door slamming. Quickly, before I could be discovered at my listening post, I eased backwards into the darkened hall and out through the dining room, where I spied my friends shedding their wet outer garments. Woods passed me from a different doorway at the back of the hall, coming from deeper within the house, going to their aid. In moments, Holmes, MacDonald, and I were all back in the sitting room, and Woods had gone to find hot drinks for the wet and weary men. I had indicated to Woods that I would also like something else to drink. He had nodded as he departed, carrying the wet coats of my friends with him.

Before I knew it, Holmes had slipped past me, following Woods to the back of the house. MacDonald and I simply looked at one another for a moment or so before we heard footsteps returning. It was Holmes, briskly rubbing his hands together.

"Forgive me," he said. "It is a little habit of mine to identify the exits of whatever building I find myself in."

MacDonald nodded knowingly. "You never do a thing without a reason, I'm thinking," he said.

Holmes simply made the beginning of a grin, and then led us toward the chairs facing the fireplace. I had started to ask him what he had learned in the village, but he obviously saw the direction of my questions and warned me with a look not to broach that subject at present. I could tell, as only someone who knew Holmes well would be able, that he had discovered something of importance that added to his satisfaction, but he did not want to share it with the Inspector. I wondered what it could be, that Holmes would wish to exclude our friend. MacDonald, facing the fire with great contentment, did not see our exchange and was not aware what he had missed. He took the chair which I had occupied during my short nap, adjusted it closer to the warming blaze, and settled in with a sigh as his long legs stretched toward the restorative flames.

Soon Woods returned, distributing glasses all around. Holmes and MacDonald were each describing where they had been when the particularly nasty portion of the storm had passed overhead. Holmes had been walking back through the village, and had taken shelter in a convenient doorway when the hail came. MacDonald had been starting up from the cottages, and had actually seen the lightning strike that had been heralded by the thunder that had awakened me.

At that moment, Burton entered from the hallway, smiling and showing no signs of his recent conversation with Mrs. Lynch. "You actually saw the strike, Inspector?

"That's right," MacDonald replied. "It struck a large elm, standing very near the stone bridge that crosses the stream before one comes to the cottages."

"Did it have a bench underneath it?"

77

MacDonald nodded. "I did see a bench in the flash of light, before I was temporarily blinded."

"Then it's unfortunate indeed that the old elm of which you speak was the one that was hit. It was one of several English elms planted by Mr. Briley when he first inherited the estate. He always referred to it as a memoriam, I assume for his father. Many is the time Mr. Briley has sat on that bench at sunset, looking out over the cottages and the estate beyond. And I sat with him there numerous times while growing up."

"Well, I'm afraid it's done for," said MacDonald, rather heartlessly in my opinion, as he appeared not to notice Burton's sadness. "There were parts of the main trunk that looked like the sap within fair boiled and exploded!" MacDonald became caught up in his description as he relived the experience, the remembered sight vivid before his eyes. "Great chunks blew out and fell to the ground, flames licking around them until the rains put them out. I've never seen anything like it!"

He finished and looked at each of us, as if expecting further comments, or perhaps a question. However, each of us was seeing it in our minds, and Burton sadly gave a short unconscious shake of his head. Finally, Holmes said quietly, *"Tempus fugit, mors venit."*

After another moment of reflection, Burton shook off his gloom and stated, "I came to let you know that Mr. Briley is awake, and will see us now."

"Excellent," said Holmes, setting aside his nearly untouched drink. MacDonald tipped his up, while mine, smaller than the one I'd had an hour or so earlier, was already gone.

We stepped across the hall, and moved toward the back of the house, passing through a doorway which I had not explored earlier. Turning right, we went along the base of the *U*-shaped building, and into a room where one of the wings turned toward the front. Knocking on the heavy door, Burton then opened it without waiting for a response and led us in to face the hostile glare of Mrs. Lynch, and the curious look from the old man sitting beside her.

Chapter 7 – Interview With The Invalid

It was a corner room, square and stretching approximately forty feet in each direction. The ceiling was higher than rooms that I had seen in the rest of the house, and the walls had a cream-colored fabric on them, looking more yellow in the gaslight than they would have on a sunny day. I could see that daylight would make the room quite cheerful indeed, with windows spaced evenly on the outside walls. Between two of the windows was a full-length glass door, covered with a curtain, and leading outside.

To our right as we entered was a large desk, with neat stacks of papers on top. Comfortable furniture was placed in several locations around the room, resting on the unusual carpet, which was predominantly red, with yellow flower patterns and limbs crisscrossing it. It also had various sigil-looking designs concealed within the larger figures, and there were very randomly placed blue patterns which, to my eye, looked vaguely piscatorial.

Two of the four walls had a number of extravagantly built bookshelves, containing hundreds of volumes of various sizes and colors. I was curious as to what sort of titles a man such as Mr. Briley enjoyed.

A molding ran around the wall at the ceiling, from which suspended wires supported paintings of various sizes and shapes. One showed three men, standing on a dock and dressed in vaguely biblical-looking red cloaks, either pointing in accusation or offering a benevolent hand (I was not sure which) toward a man lying on the ground, while a crowd looked on as the background faded into mountains and clouds. Another couple of paintings, of similar style and color, showed large buildings against a bleak sky, with minute people carrying out their business in the foreground. A sizeable painting, in an apparent place of honor to the right of the fireplace, showed a middle-aged man staring out at the viewer, his figure centered and pictured from mid-torso. He had the high collar and coat of nearly a century earlier, and side-whiskers of a different and lighter shade than the thick hair on his head. His face was clean shaven, and his clothing was an odd greenish shade, matching the right side of the background, which faded to black on the left.

The most curious thing about the painting, aside from the stern and commanding look in the subject's eyes, was the right hand. The painter had captured the man in a three-quarter pose, partially turned to his left. Although the eyes stared straight out, the head itself was turned so that the right side was more exposed. This stance allowed for the man's right hand, resting on the back of a chair, to be in full view, thus exposing the characteristic missing little finger of the Brileys.

My attention was drawn back to the two individuals waiting for us as we entered the room, but not before I saw that something about the painting had captured Holmes's special interest.

Near the fireplace, in the unique bath chair which had been mentioned by MacDonald earlier, was Mr. Martin Briley himself, and I was saddened to see the condition in which we found him. He had obviously been a man of some strength once, in spite of Burton's earlier statement that he was not a large man. He still had a frame that appeared to have some width to his shoulders. However, an exact analysis of his build was not possible, as he was completely covered by several decorative blankets, except for his head. His white hair was thinning, and the skin around his eyes was red and puffy. Although he seemed to be quite enfeebled, he did not show signs of actual illness. And yet, there was the sense that he was not long for this world, and it wasn't just my medical training that caused me to have that feeling.

Standing beside him, as if she were Cerberus, was Mrs. Lynch, a scowl on her already stern face.

"Mr. Briley can see you for five minutes," she said in a clipped tone, brooking no disagreement. Holmes flicked a glance at her, and then dismissed her as he stepped forward into Briley's immediate view.

"Mr. Briley, my name is Sherlock Holmes. This is my friend, Dr. Watson, and I understand that you spoke to Inspector MacDonald yesterday."

Briley nodded. "I've heard much about you, sir," he said, his voice stronger than one would expect. "I would have enjoyed meeting you under different circumstances."

"As would I," replied Holmes. "I've heard a great deal about you, as well as the good works you have done over the years in this community."

"Ah, Mr. Holmes, I was simply carrying out my responsibilities. Paying a debt, if you will."

"A debt," Holmes asked. "A debt to whom?"

Mrs. Lynch's brow contracted into an irate set of lines as she glanced down at Briley, but he ignored her. "It isn't important, now, Mr. Holmes," he replied. "Suffice it to say, in my youth I contracted a quantity of debt, and I have been paying it down since then. As you can see, I don't have much longer to wait for what's coming to me, and anything that I've been able to accomplish since taking over the estate has nearly come to an end. At least for me. George here," he said, nodding his head at Burton, "will be left to carry on."

"Mr. Briley," said George, with honest worry in his face, "don't talk like that! You're just going through a rough patch, sir! You'll be back up to scratch in no time!"

Briley smiled and shook his head. "I don't think so, George. But not to worry, my boy. You've always had my full confidence. You'll do what's right."

Burton turned away for a moment, leaving an awkward silence. Mrs. Lynch took that opportunity to lean over and adjust the blankets at Briley's covered shoulders.

Holmes used the pause to walk over to the painting that had previously caught his interest and study it closer. He leaned in, reading the small brass plate affixed to the bottom of the frame. "Galton Briley?" he said, looking back over his shoulder toward Mr. Briley.

"That's right," said Briley. "Painted in about 1810, when he was in his early forties."

"So this was painted a generation before you inherited the estate?"

"Yes. I was born in 1820, and he died in 1840."

"And this is a Devis?" asked Holmes, looking back up at the painting, appearing to pay special attention to the stern gaze from the figure's eyes.

"Yes, Arthur William Devis. I believe he came down from London to paint it. It's one of his lesser known works."

Holmes looked around the room, and then turned back to Briley. "Did you never have your own portrait made?" he asked.

"Never, Mr. Holmes. I've really had no interest in memorializing myself."

"But surely you would have wanted to have your picture hanging with that of your ancestor?"

Briley closed his eyes and shook his head slightly, almost without awareness. "No, Mr. Holmes. I . . . did not feel a true connection with the elder Mr. Briley. He was already in his early fifties when I was born. My mother died when I was young. Later, when I was a young man, I did not agree with some of the harsh policies he used when running the estate. When I became the master here, I worked to correct many of the things I found objectionable. I suppose that I have spent my life doing that, in this little corner of the world."

"You should not speak of such things," said Mrs. Lynch. Briley simply closed his eyes and ignored her, while Burton looked angry that she should forget her place and offer an opinion. I was interested to observe the interactions between old Mr. Briley and the housekeeper, each having lived in this house for fifty-odd years. I wondered at how tangled and knotted their relationship had become over that half-century.

83

Holmes continued to walk around the room, moving over to the outside door and attempting to look out into the darkness. He pulled aside a curtain which hung over the glass door and leaned in for a moment before letting the curtain fall back. He continued along the window to the wall, easing through the narrow space behind Mr. Briley's chair and on around to the nearby shelves.

"I observe that you enjoy the works of Charles Dickens," he said, gesturing toward a set of green leather-bound volumes at eye level. "Most of the other shelves have a thin layer of dust, both on the volumes themselves and also on the thin exposed portion of the shelf in front of the books. However, these books show signs that they are actually used on a regular basis."

Briley smiled and nodded. "You are correct, Mr. Holmes. Long ago, I read most of the books you see around us. But as the years have gone on, I found that I kept returning to my favorite volumes, as if they were visits with old friends. I had first encountered the works of Mr. Dickens when I moved up to London for a few years, in the late 1830's. He was just beginning to write, and even then he was all the rage.

"I have always regretted that I wasn't there when *The Pickwick Papers* first appeared. I would have dearly loved to have been a part of the enthusiasm from the start. But I was there as its popularity grew, and I lined up with all the rest of them to get each new issue as it was published.

"During the time I lived there in London, it seemed that I encountered many people that were exactly like the characters in Dickens' books. Many years later, I was actually able to invite him down here for a visit."

"Dickens was here?" I interrupted. As someone who also enjoyed the works of one of the nation's finest storytellers, I was interested to think that I had been in some of the same rooms where he had visited.

Briley nodded. "I think he was interested in hearing about the conditions here on the estate, and what I was trying to accomplish for the people who lived and worked here. But all that I wanted to do was talk about one of his recent books that had meant so much to me. I wish that George could have met him, but it was just a few years before he moved into the house with us."

Holmes appeared to be deep in thought for just a moment, before asking, "Would that book that meant so much to you have been *Great Expectations,* perchance?"

Briley looked surprised, but answered, "Why, yes, Mr. Holmes. But how did you know?"

"Earlier today, Mr. Burton told us a short *précis* of the events leading to his move to this house, in 1864. If Mr. Dickens visited here just a few years before that time, and you discussed one of his recent books, then most likely it was *Great Expectations,* considered one of his more notable works, and published in 1860 through 1861. His next novel, *Our Mutual Friend,* appeared from 1864 to 1865, around the time that Mr. Burton would have come to live here. Clearly, that book appeared too late to be the one in question, and incidentally it was not nearly so well regarded."

"I am impressed, Mr. Holmes. You live up to your reputation. But then, after reading Dr. Watson's account last year, I expected nothing less from you."

Holmes raised his eyebrows. "You have read that – that is to say, you've read that publication?" he said, with slight distaste. He seemed taken aback, as the experience of meeting readers of my chronicles of his investigations was still a very new thing to him at that time.

"Why, yes," said Briley. "While I mainly read the works of Dickens for personal enjoyment, I still do try to stay current." He turned his head to me. "I enjoyed the story immensely, doctor. If you wouldn't mind, could I trouble you to autograph my copy?" He nodded his head toward a shelf behind me. "If you look on the third shelf up, near that set of the works of Poe, you will see it there."

I turned and walked to the specified shelf. The small volume was there, as he had said. I noticed that while most of the shelf was covered in the thin layer of dust previously mentioned by Holmes, a half-inch or so of width in front of the book in question was wiped away. Someone had already pulled this book out, and recently.

I removed the journal, last December's *Beeton's Christmas Annual,* and held it in my hand. While it contained a number of other stories, I noted that it fell open to the first page of my own small work published within, *A Study in Scarlet.* Stepping to the nearby desk, I leaned forward and wrote, "With Best Wishes, Dr. John H. Watson." Then, I stepped to the man's bath chair and held it toward him, pages open to show my signature.

He made no effort to extricate a hand from underneath the heavy blankets, instead craning his head forward in an attempt to better see the small volume. I leaned in so that he could read the inscription. He looked at it for a moment, and then smiled and nodded. Taking that as an indication that he was through with it, I replaced it on the shelf.

"Of course," Holmes said, "there was another indication that *Great Expectations* holds some special interest for you. Earlier, during a discussion of the good work you have done here, Mr. Burton had occasion to mention Magwitch, the doomed convict from the story. He then paused for just a moment, as if the thought had some additional remembrance or significance, or had caused him to perhaps make an association. Can you think of any reason why that might have been, Mr. Briley?"

Briley's face lost its pleasant expression for a fleeting instant, and he looked over at Burton. Standing to the side, Burton had a look of puzzled embarrassment. "As I recall," he said, "the subject of Dickens was mentioned obliquely, when the Inspector said that *my life* was like something out of a Dickens story. I said that Mr. Briley was nothing like Magwitch the convict, who funded poor Pip's rise in the world to the position of young gentleman. There was nothing more to it than that.

"Ah, well," said Holmes, "I now recall that it happened exactly the way that you said. I apologize if I've caused any confusion." He paused, and added, "Or discomfort." Holmes took another step or two, looking around the room before saying, "You have done very well for yourself here, Mr. Briley. I believe that if you did feel that you had some 'quantity of debt,' as you say, to repay, then you have accomplished what you set out to do with your life. You are spoken of very highly indeed."

"I don't care what anyone thinks of me," said Briley, looking up at Holmes with an odd expression. His tone had suddenly grown slightly surly, and his good-natured mood of a moment or two earlier seemed to have evaporated. "Surely, Mr. Holmes, you haven't waited to speak to me simply to express your opinion about the way I've managed the estate over the years. Do you not have questions about the poor fellow that was found under the pipe?"

"No, none at all," replied Holmes. "I believe that much of the matter is already clear to me." Suddenly, Holmes pivoted so that he was directly facing Briley. Taking a step toward him, he said, "However, I would like to ask, if I might be so bold, if I might shake your hand."

Briley's eyes opened wider, and he looked up at Holmes in surprise. Holmes thrust out his right hand over Briley's blanketed figure and held it there expectantly. After a long moment with no response, Briley's gaze dropped, and he shook his head.

"I'm sorry, Mr. Holmes, but I cannot."

Mrs. Lynch stepped forward, almost protectively. "In Mr. Briley's condition, he cannot be exposed to anything which might compromise his teetering health."

Briley raised his eyes toward Holmes for just an instant, and then dropped them again. "I'm sure that you will understand."

"Come, Mr. Briley," said Holmes, without acknowledging Mrs. Lynch's contribution. "You are a man well known and respected for all the good works that you have done. Certainly you can have no objection to shaking my hand. After all, our opportunities for doing so are dwindling."

Briley did not raise his head. "Please show them out, Mrs. Lynch," he murmured quietly.

"Certainly," she said, with pursed lips. "Gentlemen? This way."

Holmes dropped his hand. "Well, then, perhaps another time." He turned toward the door. MacDonald and I shared a glance, and I could see that MacDonald was slightly irritated with Holmes's behavior.

Burton, with a puzzled look, said "Mr. Briley?" but Briley simply shook his head, closed his eyes, and seemed to be settling in for another nap. Burton stood for a short moment, and then turned to join us in the hall. Mrs. Lynch followed us out and pulled the door firmly shut behind her.

"Dinner will be served in just a few moments," she said. "We rarely have guests anymore, and I hope everything will be satisfactory." Her tone belied any graciousness that might have been in her words. She turned toward the rear of the house and left us standing there. As soon as she was gone, MacDonald spoke.

"I don't understand, Mr. Holmes," he said, his voice soft and his burr noticeably stronger. "I realize this is not the kind of case you usually consult upon, for Lestrade or some of the others, with a fresh corpse or life-and-death circumstances, but I thought it would be right up your alley. A body mysteriously murdered and buried before we were even born, with every indication that it is connected somehow to the family on whose estate it was found. That is just the kind of *outré* circumstance you are always telling me that you crave. And yet, when you get the chance to ask questions of the head of the household, who is old enough to have been around back when the murder was committed, who might have . . . might have . . . . " He lowered his voice even further, and said, "Forgive me Mr. Burton, but might have been *involved* in the murder, and you don't ask him *anything* of importance? Well, Mr. Holmes, I have to admit you've stumped me, and that's a fact."

Burton glared silently at MacDonald, while Holmes looked at him with a smile, and then to me. "And you, Watson? Are you 'stumped' as well?"

I considered my response for less than a heartbeat. "I *know* that this is exactly the type of investigation that you seek, Holmes. I have no question as to how you're handling things."

MacDonald quickly moved to make amends. "Well, I have no questions, as far as that goes. I have complete faith in you, Mr. Holmes. I don't think you would have come down here in this storm if you didn't want to follow up on this matter. And yet, I have to wonder at this missed opportunity."

"Perhaps it is a missed opportunity at that," replied Holmes. "We can't always play each hand with perfection, can we? If we did that, then where would be the challenge?"

MacDonald then had a new thought. "Perhaps you intend to question Mrs. Lynch, then? She's been around here fully as long as the old man. She can tell us a thing or two, I'll wager, and no mistaking it!"

Holmes shook his head. "Not yet. If the matter is still unclear, then we will speak to her about it tomorrow."

At that point, the gong was sounded, and Holmes turned toward the dining room. MacDonald and Burton shared a glance, and then both turned questioningly toward me. I raised an eyebrow in return, but could offer them no comfort. With that, Burton led us into the dining room.

Chapter 8 – A Quiet Dinner

The rain and wind outside should have given a cozy feeling to the meal, but instead, it simply seemed to add to the oppressiveness of the occasion. The food was served by the same girl who had brought our lunch. I now believed her to be Lydia, whom I had overheard being discussed by Burton and Mrs. Lynch. I looked to see if any communications passed between her and Burton, but she was quite subdued throughout the course of the meal.

The food was simple, but tasty and filling, and perfect for such a rainy night. It consisted of a hearty soup, followed by a joint of beef and roasted root vegetables. I certainly had no complaints, although I had been somewhat uneasy as to what Mrs. Lynch would provide, based on her attitude toward us all, and also because she had stated that the Shepherd's Pie from earlier in the day had been planned for the evening meal, implying that providing something for later would be a difficulty. I had been initially surprised that a residence the size of Briley House was able to function with such a small number of servants, all filling unexpected roles, but the place appeared to be run quite well. It was a testament to Mrs. Lynch, in spite of her noxious personality.

For the most part, the meal was quiet, with each of the four of us pondering our own thoughts. Burton informed us that the expectant mother had been successfully moved to the small village hospital. MacDonald tried to start a conversation, telling Burton about a case in which the three of us had been involved during the past January. It had begun on the morning after Holmes's birthday, and he had awakened in a contentious mood. Holmes normally did not acknowledge birthdays, and certainly did not celebrate them. However, he and Mrs. Hudson had conspired to try to make things a little more festive that year, in order to help me heal from the passing of Constance, little more than a week earlier. Never one for giving much weight to customs such as mourning, Holmes had tried to give me a reason to forget my sad circumstances, if only for one evening. As a result, we had both imbibed a little too much, alternating between periods of humor and morose reflection. It was after those events that MacDonald found us the next morning, to summon us to the site of a particularly grim murder.

MacDonald gamely tried to tell the story, revealing Holmes's amazing deductions regarding the coded message that Holmes had initially received from Professor Moriarty's informer, and the later significance of a missing dumbbell. However, MacDonald's narrative sputtered and died when he was trying to describe the significance of the corpse's condition, and its missing head, having been removed by a blast from a sawed-off American shot-gun. Realizing that this was a poor story for dinner, especially as he was telling this particular part while Lydia was serving dessert, he stopped altogether and simply focused on eating. I thought I saw a small smile twitch at the corner of Holmes's mouth, as he has always found humor in completely inappropriate circumstances, but I cannot be sure.

Finally, the mostly uncomfortable but perfectly edible meal came to a close, and we leaned back. Drinks were passed around for those that wanted them, and Holmes and MacDonald pulled out their pipes, with Burton's permission. MacDonald, now willing to speak again, said, "Tell us, Mr. Holmes, what did you learn when you stayed at the inn?"

Holmes pulled the pipe out of his mouth, and turned it to stare into the bowl. Satisfied that the leaf was evenly lit and burning well, he returned it and said, "We can be sure that, except for the perceptive Mr. Creed, no one else knows about the most interesting aspect of the discovered body, its missing finger, and thus the apparent connection to the Briley family. While others in the village are aware of the seeming age of the body, based on the clothing and the fact that it was found underneath the old pipe, they do not suspect anything else.

And as I said, I am confident that Mr. Creed will not reveal what he knows."

"Well, that's a relief," said Burton. "I would hate to have any scandal attach itself to Mr. Briley. In his condition, he does not need to go through something of that sort. And in spite of the Inspector's comment," he added, glancing at MacDonald, "I cannot believe that he knows anything about this. He is too good of a man for that."

"I've heard nothing but confirmation today about what a boon he has been to this community," said Holmes. "Everyone feels lucky that he made the effort to be such a good steward over the years. One of the men I spoke to after you all left was the old man by the fireplace, Abner. He affirmed all of the good work Mr. Briley has done."

"Yes, old Abner Nelson," said Burton. "He's one of our local treasures, is Abner. Many was the time when I was a boy that he would make the effort to speak with me, or explain something I did not know. And this was both before and after I came to live with Mr. Briley. It made no difference to Abner. He was always willing to take an extra minute or two. I think a lot of him, and that's the truth."

Holmes nodded, and then said, "After I left the inn, I made my way to the doctor's office. He was kind enough to summon Constable Timmons. I was able to determine to my own satisfaction that both of those men had nothing further to add, and in addition, they too will not reveal the connection of the body to the Briley family."

"I'm glad that the word hasn't gotten out about a possible family relation," said MacDonald.

"Yes, about that," said Holmes, shifting in his seat, and pulling himself a little straighter. He laid his pipe on the table and crossed his fingers on the cloth. "I would still like to be more certain in my mind about whether there is any possible family connection between the body and the Brileys. The missing finger seems an obvious link, but we can't get around the fact that there are no known legitimate or illegitimate heirs from either Mr. Briley's generation or that of his father, both men being only children. That's why I fear, Mr. Mac, that I'm going to need for you to run up to London and find the answer to these questions." He unlaced his fingers and reached into his coat, pulling out a folded set of small sheets, which I could see were covered with his fine, exact handwriting.

"Up to London, Mr. Holmes?" said MacDonald, his pipe clenched in his teeth, the end bobbing with each word. "When? Tonight? In this storm? Surely not!" There was a small throb of dismay in his voice.

"Yes, I'm afraid so. You just have time to make the last train. It is fortunate that you were able to eat before you have to leave." He handed the sheets to MacDonald, who took them and started to shuffle through each one, quickly reading the contents. "There are a series of specific questions to use when examining Briley's family connections, and who his blood kin might be, no matter how distant.

"I'll need you to go to Somerset House," continued Holmes. "You should be able to find someone to let you in, although it will be after hours, and then you can speak to a man named Dean, who is in some debt to me. He will be able to help you research the questions that I have. He has access to a number of records that, although not official, still provide a great deal of relevant information about unrecorded and less-than-legitimate family members." Picking up his pipe again, Holmes added, "Of course, you will be too late to return tonight, but we'll expect to see you in the morning."

"But . . . tonight, Mr. Holmes? In this storm?" asked MacDonald with a look of near-horror on his face. Truly, it was almost comical. When Holmes simply gave a sympathetic nod, MacDonald sighed and reached for the whisky bottle on the table. "Then at least," he said, "tell me you see a glimmer of light in this darkness."

Holmes smiled. "I do, Inspector, I do. There are some aspects that still need to be verified, but I believe that I have the correct thread in my grasp."

MacDonald nodded, and rubbed his large hand across his chin. "Any hints, then?" he asked.

Holmes thought for a moment. "As I have said," he then replied, "there is nothing new under the sun. This affair reminds me of a case that was rather similar, a matter that occurred in Nimes, thirty or so years ago."

"Quite before our time, then," said MacDonald, tipping up his glass for the last of his postprandial whiskey. With a small cough, he set it back on the table, pushed back his chair, and stood. "Then I'd best be about it." As we also stood, he waved us back, saying that there was no need to see him off, and that he knew the way to the door. With a resigned glimmer of humor in his eye, he added, "If you hadn't already had that list of questions prepared, Mr. Holmes, I might almost believe you were sending me on a wild goose chase as punishment for seeming to doubt you earlier."

Holmes smiled. "I assure you, Inspector, that the answers to those questions will have the utmost bearing on my final explanation of the case."

"Good enough, then, Mr. Holmes," said MacDonald, turning to go. In a moment, we heard the sounds of MacDonald summoning his coat and hat. Then, the front door slammed and he was gone.

We remained standing, as Burton explained that he must also leave us. "I'm going to spend the night down at the cottages, in case there are any problems associated with the flooding. I've arranged for your rooms to be fully prepared by Mrs. Lynch. Is there anything else that I can do for you before I depart?"

"As a matter of fact," said Holmes, "do you happen to have a map or drawing of the layout of the estate? I'm interested in seeing a rather complete one, if it exists. Some of the features about the place that were described to me by the locals sound rather interesting, and I thought that I might while away part of the evening studying it, if possible."

"Certainly, Mr. Holmes," said Burton. He seemed puzzled, but by this time he was certainly learning that Holmes did not say or ask anything without a reason. Within just a moment, he had returned with the map. I could see that it was simply a well-handled sketch, with various locations around the estate generally labeled in the simplest terms. It was certainly not a document of any great antiquity.

(Later, after the events of that terrible night, I was able to make a copy of Burton's map, which is appended to this manuscript. — J.H.W.)

Holmes glanced at the drawing for a moment, and then folded it along the creases that already cut through the page. He placed it in a pocket, and then stood in silence for just a moment, his arms folded, and one hand raised to his chin, a finger tapping on his lips. Burton, not quite certain what to think, glanced at me helplessly. I simply shook my head, a response that conveyed nothing at all.

Finally, Holmes seemed to come to a decision. "Mr. Burton, if I might have a word," he said. "Will you excuse us, Watson?"

I did not take any umbrage at my dismissal. I knew that Holmes, while often ignorant of some of the nuances of common social interaction, meant no offense, and that if he felt the need for an action, there was a good reason for it. I made my way into the front sitting room, where I went to stand beside the fire.

Holmes and Burton talked for only five minutes or less before rejoining me. Burton seemed to be in a rather more tense state than he had been when I had last seen him. He stated again that he needed to go to the cottages, and apologized for leaving us so early. Then, with an anxious glance toward the back of the house, and good wishes all around, he departed for the night.

Holmes pulled the map back out from his pocket and glanced at it for just a moment, before appearing to see what he was looking for. Then, ringing the bell, he said, "Would you

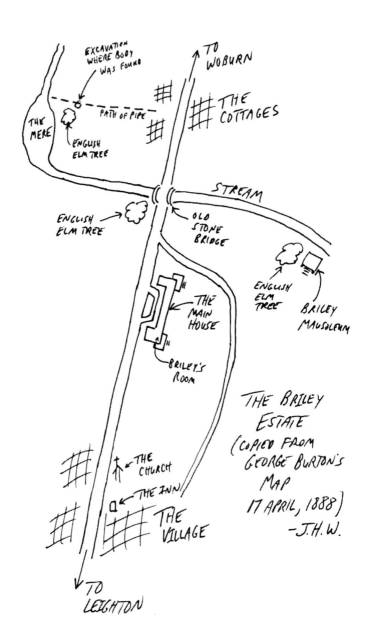

EXCAVATION
WHERE BODY
WAS FOUND

TO
WOBURN

THE
COTTAGES

THE
MERE

PATH OF PIPE

ENGLISH
ELM TREE

STREAM

ENGLISH
ELM TREE

OLD
STONE
BRIDGE

THE
MAIN
HOUSE

ENGLISH
ELM
TREE

BRILEY
MAUSOLEUM

BRILEY'S
ROOM

THE BRILEY
ESTATE
(COPIED FROM
GEORGE BURTON'S
MAP
17 APRIL, 1888)
-J.H.W.

THE
CHURCH

THE INN

THE
VILLAGE

TO
LEIGHTON

96

care to join me for a while as we smoke and discuss some things, Watson?" "Certainly," I replied, hoping that he would soon tell me the rest of the reasons why he had sent MacDonald to London.

Woods came in, and Holmes requested that we be shown to our rooms, as we were probably going to turn in. I was surprised, since it was still early. As we started to pass into the rear of the house, we encountered Mrs Lynch, standing like a guardian before the wing leading to Briley's room.

"Mr. Briley has gone to bed for the evening," she stated. "You won't be able to speak to him any further tonight."

Holmes smiled in his most charming manner and replied, "Not to worry, Mrs. Lynch. I can assure you that we will not be speaking any further to Mr. Briley during our stay, either tonight or at any other time."

Mrs. Lynch almost concealed her surprise, but not quite. She was speechless for just long enough to show that Holmes's statement had caught her off guard. No doubt she had been prepared to put up a strong argument in defense of Briley's time and health. I must admit that I, too, was not expecting to hear that we would have no further contact with the elderly invalid. Perhaps Holmes had learned enough already to explain who the mysterious dead man actually was, without further taxing the strength of the reclusive estate owner.

"Dr. Watson and I intend to turn in for the night," said Holmes, continuing as if Mrs. Lynch's awkward moment of silence had passed unnoticed. "The Inspector has returned to London, and tonight is definitely one that should be spent indoors, as I'm sure you will agree."

He cocked his head, drawing our attention to the shrieking storm, lashing rain into the nearby windows.

"Thank you again for your hospitality, Mrs. Lynch," added Holmes. "Being allowed to stay here in the house has aided our investigation substantially."

"I did not — " began Mrs. Lynch, and then she stopped herself, before beginning again. "That is to say, it was Mr.

Burton's idea that you stay here instead of down to the inn. However, as you have indicated that you have no further need to disturb Mr. Briley, I do not see any objections."

"No need at all," replied Holmes agreeably.

Mrs. Lynch nodded, her lips tight with dislike for both of us. Holmes's charm obviously counted for naught with her, but that was no surprise at all. "Then I'll wish you both good night," she said, and turned back into the wing containing Mr. Briley's room without another word.

Woods led us back into the house, but instead of turning right toward Briley's corner room, we turned left where we immediately found a wide staircase. Going up, we were led into the left wing of the house, where Woods opened a door to a sitting room, joined on either side by two bedrooms, one for each of us. He asked if there was anything else that was required.

"I'm just curious," said Holmes. "Where do the other occupants of the house sleep?"

"There are very few other occupants at present," replied Woods. I had noticed that he had a certain forwardness about him that did not seem intimidated at all by either being in the presence of strangers, or the formality supposedly required by his position. "Mr. Burton sleeps in this wing, just down the hall. Mrs. Lynch has a corner room in the south wing, directly upstairs over Mr. Briley's room. The rest of the servants are either in the basement or near the kitchen."

"So Mrs. Lynch does not sleep with the servants?" said Holmes.

"No, sir. She's more like the lady of the house than a servant." Woods made this statement with the faintest hint of judgment. Holmes did not let it pass.

"Aren't you taking something of a chance, saying such things to total strangers? After all, you work under the direction of Mrs. Lynch. It would probably not be wise to get on her bad side."

"I'm not afraid," said Woods. "Mr. Burton knows how she is, and if she tried to get back at me, he would make sure that I still had a job in the village, even if she did get me moved out of the house. We've all seen how she tries to treat him, and how he stands up to her. She's been that way for years. Everyone around here knows just how far her power goes.

"And in any case," he added, "she can't live forever, and when my sister is the lady of the house, I'll be helping to run the estate myself, I expect, and then whatever Mrs. Lynch thinks won't matter at all."

"Your sister?" asked Holmes, but I interrupted.

"Of course, I should have seen it," I said. "Your sister — "

" — is the girl that has served our meals," finished Holmes. "I noticed the resemblance immediately, as I'm sure did Dr. Watson."

I had not. "Her name is Lydia," I added. "George Burton intends to marry her."

Holmes looked at me with amused surprise. "Clearly, we each have items to report to one another." Turning to Woods, he said, "That will be all, I think. And Woods?"

Woods, who had been reaching for the door, turned. "While your situation may seem protected at present, it would probably still be wise to avoid running afoul of Mrs. Lynch. I can assure you that it would not be wise to cross her."

Woods looked back in silence as these words sank in. Then, with a nod, he turned and left the room.

Holmes turned to me and said, "Let us sit and smoke for a while, Watson. We have time to discuss some things, before our investigation resumes."

Chapter 9 – The Calm During The Storm

Holmes gestured toward the two armchairs located near the fire. I knew that he wished to use me as his sounding board, as he had so often in the past. By discussing the case with me, he would be able to arrange his thoughts in such a way as to order them from start to finish. Occasionally, I might ask a question which would reveal to him an aspect of the matter that might not have previously been considered.

After the travels of the day, the tramps through the rain, and the recent meal in the warm room downstairs, I wished that I was going to be dozing in front of the fire instead of discussing the case. Clearly, however, Holmes had something else planned for the night, and now was not the time to rest. We settled in, one on each side of the fire, mirroring our usual arrangement in the Baker Street sitting room. After taking time to prepare our pipes, we were at last ready to speak.

"I take it," said Holmes, "that you have gained some knowledge of Burton's plans for his future. I had noticed you were watching both him and the serving girl at dinner more closely than I would have expected, and certainly with more attention than you showed them during lunch."

I proceeded to relate the conversation that I had overheard before Holmes and MacDonald had arrived back at the house. In times past, I would have felt some hesitance and reluctance about eavesdropping as I had, as well as unhesitatingly reporting on what I had heard. However, I had long ago found that all was fair when conducting an inquiry with Holmes, and I also knew one might not realize which particular fact would be the key that would unlock the door, thus allowing Holmes to complete his case. Therefore, I always kept my eyes and ears open, and reported what I had learned as best as I could. It had paid off more often than not, especially during the recent events of the Shropshire House, and the wily counterfeiters who had ensconced themselves within it.

"I had suspected as much," said Holmes, "and it is well for Burton that it appears to be no secret. If Mrs. Lynch knows about and disapproves of it, you may be certain Briley also knows about it. And since there seems to be no disappointment coming from that direction, one may assume Briley approves of the match. That is significant, since it is almost certain that Burton is the man's heir, in spite of there being no known written acknowledgement of the fact."

"And you believe Burton when he states that he does not *know* if he is the heir?"

"Provisionally."

"Is the lack of a written record regarding Briley's heir one of the facts that you confirmed while in the village this afternoon?"

"It was alluded to in an oblique fashion by several of the individuals that I encountered. At one point while I was at the inn, I managed to turn the conversation toward Burton. He is very well thought of, and I could not get any sense that anyone wishes him ill will. The story of his rescue as an orphan by Briley is well known, and there is no resentment associated with it at all. It is also common knowledge that Burton's cap is set on Lydia Woods, and the feeling is that it will be a fine match.

"She is a village girl, now in her early twenties, hired several years ago to work in the house. One of Briley's characteristics has been to provide places in service in his home for the young people of the area. Whatever one may say of Mrs. Lynch and her thorny disposition, she runs a smart household, and her staff is well-trained. If they decide to leave for other positions elsewhere, in London for instance, or at another country home, they are given excellent references."

I pulled on my pipe, which had reached that perfect point of fulmination, evenly lit and drawing well. As Holmes discussed Burton, I considered if this was the time to ask why he had pulled the young man aside after dinner. I chose to let the matter rest, realizing that Holmes would only share with me what had been discussed if and when he was ready.

After a moment or two of thought, I asked instead, "Will you not tell me the real reason for sending poor MacDonald back to London on such a night? I cannot conceive that you had such an urgent need of information regarding the Briley family that you couldn't have sent the man in the morning. Or you could have simply sent a wire to Dean in London, for that matter."

Holmes shook his head. "I assure you, Watson, that a quick trip to London is exactly what I needed from the Inspector. Of course, I intend to act before he returns, no matter what results he brings with him. What he discovers, however, may or may not help me to realize whether I've made the correct decision."

"So you have reached a solution to the matter?" I asked. "Was it from something that was conveyed to you this afternoon, after we left you in the village?"

"Actually, I had a fairly certain idea of the basic framework of the events that took place some fifty years ago before we ever left this house for the village."

"And are you ready to reveal the entire truth to me?" I asked.

Holmes smiled, shook his head, and said, "Not until I have answered all my questions to my own satisfaction." Then, he continued by saying, "My conversation with Abner, the old man by the fireplace, added a few additional brushstrokes of confirmation to the canvas, and the meeting with Mr. Briley after that fairly completed the picture. There is one other verification you and I must make tonight, Watson, just to sew up a loose end, or paint in the last corner, to complete my metaphor, and I apologize in advance, as it will certainly be unpleasant at best."

"And then, when the entire matter is clear to you, you may or may not share your results with MacDonald?" I asked. "It is, after all, his case, Holmes, and he summoned you here to provide assistance. Do you believe that you can suppress the truth of these events, whatever they turn out to be?"

He thought for a moment, letting his gaze drop reflectively toward the low fire. He seemed to be thinking carefully. Finally, he spoke, stating softly, "A quantity of debt, Watson, a quantity of debt."

"What?" I said. "That was what Briley said earlier. What does it mean?"

"Watson, have you read *Great Expectations*?" he asked.

I felt as if I was suddenly lost in high weeds, but I responded, "Yes, some years ago."

"What do you recall about it?"

"Well, it is the story of a young boy, Pip, who is the narrator of the tale. He lives in poverty, but has aspirations for something better. One day he helps an escaped convict named Magwitch. Then he becomes associated with a mad-woman named Miss Havisham, and falls in love with her adopted daughter, Estella."

My enthusiasm began to warm as I remembered more of the book. "Later, he is taken to London and made into a gentleman. He hopefully believes this has been done by Miss Havisham, but in fact it is due to the secret manipulations of the grateful convict, who in the intervening years was transported and subsequently made a fortune. Pip encounters Magwitch, who has returned secretly to London, and by that point he has gotten into debt from his extravagant lifestyle — "

"Your memory of the story is excellent," interrupted Holmes. "Having recalled that much, then you may remember that after young Pip moves to London, he uses the phrase 'a quantity of debt' to describe how he has begun to live with a buy-now and pay-later attitude. The lesson is, of course, that at some point, the debt must be paid.

"There have been times, Watson, especially when I was younger, when I felt upon looking back that my solution to one case or another may have caused more harm than good. I have occasionally dragged certain matters into the light of day that should have remained in darkness, because I was too interested in proving I was right, when I should have stepped back for a moment to consider the greater benefit of silence. I can assure you that later, when I had an opportunity to reflect upon my actions after the truth was irretrievably exposed, I regretted that I did not stay my hand.

"On those few occasions, I have caused more harm than good by revealing a solution in order to improve my reputation, or as a sop to my immediate vanity. My younger self was building up a quantity of debt I am sometimes forced to pay now by being more judicious with my conclusions. I have learned that occasionally justice should be tempered and dispensed in due moderation."

"And are you the person to decide?" I asked. "When it should be tempered?"

"Possibly. I have no official standing here, and my conclusions are my own. My perspective is from the outside looking in, so I do not see issues as one of the Yarders would. I can only try to balance the crime versus the greater good. And luckily, I have you, my friend, to help guide me at times as a moral compass."

"But surely, Holmes, when one considers murder versus some greater good . . . . " I let my voice trail off. I felt glad that he counted on me, but at the same time, I questioned whether I wanted to share any of the responsibility that he was taking upon his own soul.

Finally, after we had smoked in silence for some further minutes, he sighed and stated, "In this particular case, I must admit I'm not at all certain how justice can be exacted without also punishing the innocent. That factor weighs on my decision."

"Do you feel that punishment is still possible for the crime we are now investigating, even after all the years that have passed since the poor fellow from the trench was murdered?"

"Yes, but I may have to reveal more of my cards than I would wish in order to force my opponent to do so as well."

"I believe that I am beginning to have a vague understanding of the direction that your thinking is leading, Holmes. After all, there have no doubt been many cases whereupon a man, wracked by guilt for the crime of murder, no matter how secretly he manages to hide it, then spends a lifetime trying to atone for it with good works. Do not forget that it was Briley who first mentioned the idea of 'a quantity of debt.' "

"So you have fixed Mr. Briley as the murderer of the man buried beneath the pipe?"

"Is that not what you have implied?" I asked.

"I did not say so," said Holmes.

"But surely that would explain things? Fifty years ago, give or take, a man arrives who is somehow connected to the Briley family. Perhaps he was an illegitimate son, fathered by Mr. Briley's father. Let us say that he was older than Mr. Briley, and, in spite of his illegitimacy, he had some sort of document proving that he was the legitimate heir. Then, Mr. Briley, either with calculated cunning, or perhaps in a fit of rage, kills the visitor. He manages to hide the body until he can institute the installation of the pipe from the cottages down to the mere. Realizing it would be a perfect hiding place, he buries the body, where under almost any circumstances it would be unlikely ever to be excavated again. Little does he suspect that the nature of the soil there will mummify it, or that his ward, fifty years later, will take it upon himself as part of his duties while running the estate to make repairs in that same area, revealing the evidence of the long suppressed crime."

"And what if I tell you that, contrary to common belief now, I have it on good authority that the pipeline was actually begun by Mr. Briley's father, Galton, a month or so *before* the old man died and Martin Briley subsequently inherited the estate?"

"You learned this from Abner, I suppose?"

Holmes nodded. "Then it changes nothing," I said. "In fact, it makes it easier for Martin Briley to have done as I've described. After Briley killed the illegitimate visitor, he knew exactly where he could hide the body, since there was already open excavation taking place on the estate that he believed would never again be opened."

"It is an interesting theory, and there is much about it that fits the facts. And there is something else you have not thought of that, when viewed from your perspective, might tend to support the interpretation you have constructed. Do you see it?"

I thought for a moment, and then possibly longer, only drawn back to myself when some of the coal in the fireplace collapsed in upon itself. And then I spotted it.

"Mrs. Lynch!" I said. "Of course! If Mr. Briley *did* do the murder, somehow she knew about it, too, and has used it to blackmail him all these years, setting herself up as the queen of her little kingdom here in the house. Mr. Briley, feeling guilty for what he had done, has tried for the rest of his life to make up for his actions by being a benevolent figure to everyone under his influence, paying off his perceived quantity of debt. He has opposed Mrs. Lynch as he could, but only when truly necessary, picking his battles, but otherwise letting her act as if this were actually *her* home as much as his. In fact, she referred to it as *'my house'* when she was arguing with Burton!"

Holmes nodded. "That is certainly one way of looking at it," he said, "although I don't subscribe to that view. You are like a man riding on a train, looking over into a carriage traveling side-by-side on a parallel track. While some of the events occurring within it are clear for a moment, from your single fixed view, there is more to what is happening in the other carriage than you can possibly know for certain. And there is more to this matter than you are taking into account."

"Are you implying that there has been some illicit relationship between Martin Briley and Mrs. Lynch?"

"No, I'm certain that has not been the case."

"Then what, exactly, do you know that I do not, which prevents me from making an accurate assessment?"

"I know very little more, and some aspects must remain hidden at present, pending verification. I will tell some of it to you now, however. For instance, I have obtained information from old Abner, who is in his eighties, older than we first thought. He recalls certain facts relating to the events that occurred here at the time of the death of old Mr. Galton Briley. But as I say, these facts only tend to confirm what I have already suspected. By the time we had set out for the inn this afternoon, you had also seen what I had seen. After I returned, you did not have the advantage of having heard Abner's story, but after we interviewed Mr. Briley in his chambers, you had at that point seen all of the physical evidence that I, myself, had also witnessed."

"Seen, but not observed, apparently," I said, without rancor. I was far too used to that feeling to have any bitterness about it. "And is that why you chose not to ask Mr. Briley any questions? It was because you had already seen *and* observed enough to confirm your theories?"

"Exactly. I will confess that there was the case rather like this in Nimes, thirty or so years ago, that suggested itself soon after we examined the body. The exact date of that crime escapes me. I had thought of having MacDonald stop by our rooms to examine my indexes to confirm it, but I decided it would be wiser if he did not. Perhaps I should not have mentioned it to him at all, but in any case he seemed uninterested once he realized that it took place long ago.

"In spite of the fact that I cannot recall specifics of the matter, what I had observed here was enough to convince me that my supposition was correct, and that these events are laid out on lines of a similar course."

"And just so I'll be caught up," I said, "first will you now tell me what you learned from Abner?"

"With great pleasure, my dear Watson. It will help pass the time of this rainy evening until the next act of our drama."

107

He rose, threw another lump of coal on the fire, and returned to his seat. As he went again through the pipe-lighting ritual that I knew so well, I listened to the wind throwing sheets of water from the storm against the walls of the house. I pitied anyone out on a night such as this. Little did I anticipate what plans Holmes would propose when our quiet discussion was eventually completed.

"Old Abner is a beloved fixture in the village. He is enjoying a well-earned rest now, due to the charity and good works of Martin Briley, who has made certain that the old folks here are cared for in their later years. Abner has spent most of his life working in the estate stables, having started there when he was just a boy, back during the War of the Fifth Coalition."

I thought for a moment, as Holmes looked at me patiently. "If memory serves," I said, "that was in 1809, when we fought with Austria against Napoleon and his alliance with Bavaria."

"Very good, Watson."

"That makes Abner a very old man indeed."

"True. Abner told me that he was nine years old at the time he came to the stables, meaning he was born in 1800. As I said, the man is older than we initially thought, which says much for the restorative powers of country living, and he is still as sharp as a tack."

"Hold for just a moment, Holmes," I interrupted. "Are you not the man who chided me during the early days of our friendship by saying that a man's brain is like an empty attic, and only a fool takes in every sort of lumber, so that what might actually be useful to him must be crowded out? I believe you indicated that it was a mistake to believe that your brain-attic, as you called it, would stretch to hold every useless fact, and that eventually something of importance would be lost? You refused to acknowledge the Copernican Theory, for God's sake! How can you know about an obscure little war that was part of a series of other obscure little wars?"

Holmes's eyes glinted with a merry light. "We have surely established by now that I actually *do* believe that all knowledge might useful, at some point or other. The conversation that you recall, and which is now permanently and unfortunately memorialized in your publication of last winter, must have been on a day when I was feeling particularly querulous. I was certainly tweaking you, but you did not know me well enough then to realize it. And as far as knowing about the events of the Fifth Coalition, well, it is just possible that it *may* have had relevance in a previous case of mine, and perhaps I had an ancestor who fought in it."

I sat forward. "If it *was* one of your earlier cases, I would very much like to have a record of it for my notes."

"Ah, Watson, that would be a story for another time. For now, let us return to the matter before us, and the tale of Abner the Stable Hand."

Sadly realizing that he was not going to elaborate on that other case at the present time, and if I brought it up again at some future point he might not wish to discuss it, I released myself from its pull and settled back to resume our discussion of the venerable Abner.

"As I was saying, Abner was born in the village in 1800, and went to work in the house stables when he was nine years old. He recalls the events very clearly, even for a fellow of his age. In those days, Galton Briley was a hard man, intent on building his fortunes. And not long after Abner started his life's work in the stables, Galton Briley took a wife.

"Abner told me the estate was a much different place at that time. By then, Galton Briley was about forty years old, and had been living in this house where we are sheltering tonight for about twenty years, having built it in the very late 1700's. Upon the death of his father, the original founder of the fortune, Galton Briley had taken his father's money, made from a series of profitable shipping ventures, and had wisely invested it. This had allowed him to buy up a great deal of the land here. He eventually built a great estate, encompassing the village and a number of surrounding farms, stretching to the north almost to the lands around Woburn Abbey.

"Galton had found a girl in London and brought her back here. Abner remembers her as a sad young thing, quite a bit younger than her husband, less than half his age. Abner only recalls seeing her on rare occasions, but stated that she always appeared to have a grim cloud about her. She stayed inside most of the time, and there were no visitors to the house, ever.

"Even out in the stables, they were aware that Galton Briley's fortunes were increasing by leaps and bounds, and yet the Briley family had a marked unhappiness about it. This continued until 1820, more than a decade after Abner started working here. At that time, the house went through a period of subdued excitement, as the first and only child of Galton Briley was born. Abner recalls it was not celebrated as it ought to have been, due to both Galton Briley's grim disposition, and also due to the fact that his wife was in ill health after the birth, a condition that plagued her until her death.

"Abner did not recall the exact date it occurred, but Martin Briley's mother died within a year or so of his birth. I was able, while returning from the village, to stop in and check the parish records, which confirmed that she passed in 1822."

"You made good use of your time," I said.

"Indeed. It was the church doorway in which I sheltered during the hail storm."

"When you described the incident earlier, when we were with MacDonald, I recall you did not mention that fact."

"You are correct. It would be wise to keep a close hand on our cards at present, as you will no doubt see later tonight, if all goes according to plan."

"So you expect this matter to be resolved this evening?"

"I do," replied Holmes.

"And getting MacDonald away and up to London is part of the plan."

"Yes. As I've implied, depending how the results of tonight's events turn out, it might do more harm than good for the officials to learn what we will find. But to return to Abner's story."

He pulled deeply on his pipe, and resumed. "Galton Briley was a hard man, but not necessarily a bad man, in the sense that he did not do evil just for the sake of evil. However, he assuredly was *not* considered a good man, and he was mostly interested in profit, often to the point of neglecting the people under his care. Abner did not fare too badly in his position, working so near the house. But some of the estate folk had a meager life indeed.

"You must remember that back in those days, the early decades of the century, very few people were rewarded with the type of lives that some of us are fortunate enough to have today. A roof over one's head and knowing where some — but not all — of your next meals were coming from was usually good enough. People did not tend to stray from their localities, or move off to London without a very good reason.

"And so, having set the scene, some of our more familiar characters start to take the stage. Abner related to me that there was a family in the village at this same time, a shiftless bunch that always maintained a rather unpleasant reputation. He was not sure about the exact date, but some years after he went to work in the stables, that family had a daughter. The family's name was Lynch."

Holmes paused, watching me to see if felt the need to comment, and I responded. "A daughter named Lynch. Is she somehow related to that most winning woman, Mrs. Lynch, who has graced us with her presence today?"

"The fact of the matter is, the woman we know as Mrs. Lynch is actually the same woman. She has never married."

"Never married?" I asked. "So like many housekeepers who never marry, she goes by the sobriquet of *Mrs.* as a badge of office."

"Precisely. I believe, from my conversation with Abner, that she gradually assumed that exact title over the years in order to avoid confusion and maintain her authority as the housekeeper. It seems that she is a piece of work, is our Mrs. Lynch, and she started on it early.

"Abner related to me that Mrs. Lynch, or Elizabeth, as she was known then, came to work in this house in around 1830, when he had been here over twenty years. By then he was a full-fledged member of the little family that comprised the staff, and he was in a position to watch as young Elizabeth started her steady rise to housekeeper. Abner was married by this point, and his wife also worked in the house, so he was able to hear about the girl's steady progress.

"Elizabeth Lynch began as a scullery maid, and within just a couple of years, had risen to the unlikely position of head housekeeper, while just in her early twenties. Of course, the estate was scandalized, but she had been chosen by Galton Briley, and she had his authority behind her. One fine day the previous housekeeper was sent on her way, Elizabeth became Miss Lynch, and she began to run the house as it pleased her. Old Galton, then in his early sixties, simply sat back and let her.

"On some occasion after Miss Lynch had begun her long reign over the house, young Martin Briley departed from the scene. He had never been much involved with the estate during the entire time he was growing up, staying in the house, while his father went about and carried out the running of the place. There was never any sign that Martin was being trained to take over the management of either the estate or any of his father's other affairs. In the last years before Martin, while still a boy it seems, took himself off to London, there were rumors of bitter rows between him and his father in the house. Abner's wife told him what she knew, but it wasn't everything. All that Abner recalled was that one day, Martin Briley left for London, and his father started his slow decline, spending more and more time withdrawn in the house, while Miss Lynch expanded her influence.

"Over the years, as the generations came and went, the *Miss* became *Mrs.*, possibly as the newer and younger servants simply assumed that she had once been married. She must have allowed it, or perhaps seen its usefulness, as that is how she now refers to herself. Very few people other than Abner probably even recall any of her early history, or the fact that she has never been married. As for Abner's wife, she died while giving birth to their only child, along with the baby. He understandably had less interest in the doings of the house for quite some time after that point."

Holmes paused to stare at the fire for a moment, and then said, "And now we come to the most important part of the story. In the spring of 1840, nearly this time of year according to Abner, old Galton Briley, who had not been seen for months as he languished in this building, finally succumbed to old age. The odd thing is that, until Martin Briley showed up at the house, after having been gone for a number of years, the people of the estate did not even realize that the old man had died. Mrs. Lynch, as we shall now resume calling her, had prepared the body on her own, and had given her staff no indication whatsoever that anything was amiss.

"Abner recalls that one morning, there was simply an announcement from Mrs. Lynch that Martin Briley had returned to the estate, claiming his inheritance following the death of his father. Nothing had been seen or heard from Martin in several years, and suddenly he was back home, in the house, his arrival unnoticed by Abner or any of the staff.

"Abner stated that no one had any knowledge regarding Martin's activities in London. Oh, there had been rumors of wild living, debauchery, and extravagant use of his father's money over the past few years, but nothing was ever confirmed. And now the prodigal had returned.

"Mrs. Lynch gave everyone to understand that a private burial of the old man had already occurred in the family mausoleum, which had been built in the early 1820's, a year or so before the time of Martin Briley's mother's passing, in preparation for her impending death, as it was expected at the time that she would die earlier rather than later. No one was invited to pay their respects to Galton Briley. Mrs. Lynch related that an ancient clergyman from another village had been found to read a few words over the body, and the service, such as it was, had been attended solely by Mrs. Lynch before Martin Briley had been able to return. No subsequent memorial service was held in the church for any of the locals to attend, and truth be told, they had no interest in attending one.

"Thus, Galton Briley was laid to rest in the mausoleum, with his departed young wife, the only two occupants of the structure. And the only witness was Mrs. Lynch, the young housekeeper."

Holmes gave me a moment to digest what he had told me before continuing. "After the funeral, Martin Briley spent several months shut up in the house. Any instructions from him to the estate manager were conveyed by Mrs. Lynch. A number of cosmetic improvements were begun at that time, and they continued over the next several years, eventually making the house much more attractive and livable than it had been during the final years of Galton Briley's life."

"But," I asked, "how was Mrs. Lynch able to accomplish all this out without anyone questioning her?"

"You must remember that in those days, this was a much more remote area. There was no adequate law enforcement in existence. And Mrs. Lynch had spent several years building up her authority, as given to her by Galton Briley. Finally, the heir had returned to the house, and even though he wasn't seen for several months, Mrs. Lynch was presumably speaking for him when she provided direction to the estate manager and the staff.

"Finally, as the summer was turning to fall of 1840, Martin Briley began to emerge from his self-imposed hibernation. He started to take an interest in the affairs of the estate, which had been in the capable hands of the old estate manager hired years earlier by Galton. Martin apprenticed himself to the fellow, working to learn every aspect of the running of the place, and unafraid to get dirty as he did so. He began to make a number of substantial improvements to the living quarters of his tenants, and we've heard how over the years he also endeared himself to the locals with his progressive efforts toward maintaining good schools and medical care, and so on. He also reversed a number of Galton Briley's oppressive conditions related to tenancy agreements."

"A quantity of debt," I said.

"Indeed. Interestingly, Martin Briley is now often credited with the plumbing improvements and the installation of the pipe where the body was discovered two days ago, but as I said, that was originally an improvement begun by the estate manager during Galton's final days, not because of any benevolent concern for the living conditions of the cottagers. Rather, it was due to the fact that whatever drainage system there was or was not in place before that time was leading to disease that was affecting the workers, and thus the prosperity of the estate as a whole."

I thought for a moment about what Holmes had related to me. Nothing in what he had said contradicted with my earlier theory, and I told him so. "Again, I state that nothing that you have said negates my interpretation of what we have seen. An illegitimate Briley heir could have arrived, and Martin killed him to protect his inheritance. I had first believed that Mrs. Lynch gained her ascendance by blackmailing Martin, but I now see that she was already on her throne during Galton's lifetime. Whatever seamy arrangement had caused Galton to elevate her to the position of head housekeeper might not have been enough to influence Martin the same way. But if she had some hold over him in the form of knowledge about the murder he had committed, then that would be enough to assure that she would *continue* to maintain her position."

"Ah, Watson," said Holmes. "You are stubborn yet. But you are still not taking into account the things which you have seen today."

"Seen, but not observed," I said.

"Exactly."

I did not reply for a moment, and then asked, "And was there something in Abner's story which guided you toward the truth?"

"There is nothing definite that caused me to suddenly see these events with a new and unexpected clarity. As I mentioned, I already had a vague idea of what had occurred those many years ago. Abner simply helped me to focus some of the details, as did my examination of the information in the parish records."

An obvious thought occurred to me. "Holmes? Do you think that Mrs. Lynch had something to do with the death of old Galton Briley, those many years ago?"

He took his pipe from his mouth, and turned it so as to see into the bowl. The flame must have finally gone out, for he set it aside. "It is possible, Watson, and we may actually find out more about that part of the tale later tonight. However, it is incidental to the facts relating to the dead man found under the pipe. *That* is the question we can definitely answer. Although," he added, "I'm still of an uncertain mind as to what effect the answer will have. I cannot see a satisfactory solution, and I'm afraid we will have to let events run their course, once we nudge them into motion. And that, my friend, is a situation that is never the preferred option. Like a good solicitor, one should already know the answer before one asks the question. That way there will be no surprises."

He then stood up. "And sadly, Watson, you still haven't asked all of the right questions. But all will be made clear."

"Tell me, then, what is one of the questions that I should be asking?"

"Why, what I meant when I mentioned earlier that our discussion would pass some of the time until the next act of our drama. But now, there is no need to ask, for the curtain is about to rise. I believe that we have talked long enough that the household has settled, and all people with clear consciences, and a few without them as well, are now in for the night.

"Come, Watson, let us return to the storm. We have one more grim errand to perform, and then we shall have everything we need to present our case."

Chapter 10 – The Grim Errand

I had dreaded this moment, as I saw Holmes moving on silent feet toward the door to the hallway. I understood that he wished to move quietly, taking no chances of waking the house. He carefully opened the door and stepped out, expecting me to follow.

The hall was lit by a dim glow, where shadows could be avoided but not identified. Holmes moved like a cat, carefully placing each foot, in spite of the solid flooring which gave every indication that it would not creak or groan at an inopportune moment. I followed him as best I could, and I felt that I acquitted myself well, considering the aches in my leg that had been aggravated by the terrible weather.

Holmes led me to a set of back stairs at the left-hand side of the house, where the servants slept. On the ground floor, he unerringly found the alcove where our coats were hung. Woods had done his best to arrange them so that they would dry, but, as I had feared, they were still quite damp. I would be lucky to escape this particular adventure without a full-blown case of pneumonia. I feared that we were both heading for pesky spring colds, at best.

With a sigh, I followed Holmes out of a rear door, onto a stone-floored landing. I could sense more than see the rain drops dashing into the standing puddles all around us. "Leave the door on the latch," whispered Holmes, as he turned toward a set of steps leading down from the landing to the grounds below.

Away from the protection of the house, the wind found us. I clutched my coat tighter, wishing that I had dressed more for winter than spring. There was an iciness to the water that found its way under my hat and coat.

We were at least fifty yards from the house, as we traversed the wide sloping lawn at the rear, when Holmes paused and looked back. I also turned, and saw that the massive structure standing above us was no more than a looming black shadow. However, to our left, at the base of the great house, a pair of rooms showed lights. One, on what would be the ground floor, and another one floor above it. The ground floor room appeared to have a door which opened onto a landing similar to the one that we had just used to exit the building.

"Mr. Briley's room," said Holmes with a gesture, "and that is Mrs. Lynch's there above him. It seems that neither can sleep tonight."

"Perhaps, as Mr. Briley's room is something of a sick chamber, a light is left burning throughout the night, in case he needs assistance."

"Possibly," said Holmes. "We shall see."

A thought occurred to me. "When you returned to the house this afternoon, you followed Woods into the back of the house. Was that when you determined where the rear entrance was located? And also where our coats were being kept?"

"Of course. As I told MacDonald, it has always been a habit of mine to identify the exits of whatever building in which I find myself."

"And the map you requested from Burton? Was it to locate our current destination?"

"Exactly, Watson. As for now, let us continue on our quest. What we have to do is not going to get any more pleasant by putting it off."

At that moment, lightning flashed, followed by a roll of thunder a few seconds later. "The storm is returning," said Holmes, needlessly.

"Then let us get this over with," I said. Gesturing, I added, "After you."

We set off down the rest of the gentle slope, stepping carefully so as not to lose our footing on the wet grass, or stride into some unseen depression. I had glanced at the map provided to Holmes earlier in the evening, and was starting to have an idea of our destination, although I could not yet understand the purpose.

We were now far enough away from the house that the lights from the bedrooms were no longer visible. There had been a few more flashes of lightning, but they were in the distance. However, the wind was blowing from that direction, and I knew the storm was steadily moving our way.

We were rounding a small copse that had been allowed to grow up through some ragged boulders when Holmes grabbed my arm and pulled me into the deeper shadows. For a moment I did not understand, and then I heard it too. It was the sound of a carriage, making its way from our left, the direction of the stream and the cottages.

Gradually it came closer, the rhythm of the horses' hooves hitting the wet ground more felt than heard. I could see now that the carriage was rolling across a rough track that ran along the bottom of the hill. We had been about to cross it before Holmes stopped me, and I had not even realized it was there.

My eyes had finally adjusted to the night, especially after leaving the influence of the bedroom lights that we had turned and seen earlier, and now I could recognize details of the carriage. It was closed, with the driver sitting high on top, his hands gripping the reins as the horse moved steadily forward, but not too quickly. Just as it was passing in front of us, I recognized the driver. It was George Burton.

Sitting inside the carriage was another figure, with a pale face pressed to the window. Before I could recognize who it was, they were gone, down the track which undoubtedly led back in the direction of the village. The sounds faded away, and we were left with the familiar rain and wind once again.

"Holmes," I whispered, as if someone were out there to hear us, "what is he doing? He said he would spend the night down at the cottages, in case his help was needed should there be flooding. Do you suppose that there has been an emergency?"

"Perhaps," Holmes replied. "However, I fancy a somewhat different explanation, and I'm certain that all shall be made clear in the morning. I hope I am right, and that there still may be some sort of happy ending out of this whole nasty business. However, Burton's midnight ride does not affect in the least what we are doing right now. Pray, let us continue."

And with that, he stepped out and across the track without another word. I moved to catch up with him. We continued on down the gentle slope, and I knew from studying the map that if we kept going, we would eventually reach the stream at a location before it dropped and wound around the cottages and emptied through the mere. I believed, however, that we would reach our destination before we came to the stream, and in just a few more minutes, I was proved right.

We stopped on a low rise, near a wooded area that looked down on the water below us. It was simply a deeper black in the night around us, but I could hear the rush of the waters as they tumbled and lost elevation while speeding along the stream bed. Then my attention turned back to our goal. It was a small building, probably no more than twenty by twenty, and made of such white marble that it even seemed to shine weakly in the dark night. It was only a single story, with one heavily decorated metal door centered in the front wall. The corners of the small building were simulated Doric columns, incorporated within the walls, and supporting the gently sloped roof, also made of marble. A pair of Corinthian columns stood on either side of the door, and a small porch was reached by four very shallow marble steps.

Nearby was a lone tree, set apart from the others. It looked to be an elm, and at its base was a marble bench, consisting simply of a couple of side supports, and topped by a flat slab. In better weather, it would provide a lovely view out over the stream toward the cottages and farms.

Holmes did not see it that way. "A rather lonely spot," he said, stepping carefully up onto the porch, while fumbling under his Inverness coat for something. "Do be careful," he said. "These steps slope down from front to back, allowing water to pool along the risers. They also appear to have settled in the years since the building was constructed, and they are quite slick."

I paid heed to his warning, and followed him onto the porch, where he was in the process of lighting a dark lantern. Then, with the opening narrowed to the thinnest possible slit, he bent and began to manipulate his splendid set of pick-locks into the mausoleum door.

I knew that any remonstrance I might make about what we were about to do would fall upon deaf ears. Holmes was on the track, like a hound that had taken the scent, and if he needed a fact to complete his case, then nothing would stand in his way. After some of the objectionable situations in which he and I had found ourselves over the years, such as the Dreadful Tragedy of the Powys Stone, I knew that there was almost nothing I could say which might dissuade him from his task. Even if, assuming that I was correct, that task involved desecration of a corpse.

It occurred to me, while Holmes worked on the lock, that I had not mentioned something that I had previously noticed. I explained how the dust had been disturbed in front of the copy of *Beeton's*, which had contained my own recently published story. "What do you think it means?" I asked.

"Possibly Mr. Briley simply refreshed his memory when it was announced that you and I would be arriving to make inquiries," he whispered, as he worked in darkness to feel the inner workings of the lock. "Or perhaps, he wanted to see what sort of opponents he might be facing." Then, with a triumphant but whispered, "A-ha!" Holmes straightened up and stepped back. The door had opened.

It had been but the work of a moment for Holmes to turn the lock in the heavy door. "Child's play," he muttered. "They think that just because it needs a great heavy key, it provides some extra protection. The larger the lock, the easier it is to feel the works."

He pushed the door open. The wind seemed to die at that moment, and a musty, yet not totally unpleasant, odor, reached us from the still air within. "It is ventilated," said Holmes. "There are often small gaps designed between the walls and the roof to allow the building to breathe. Otherwise, the decay of the bodies within would be intolerable whenever the building had to be reentered."

He widened the opening a little further and stepped in. I followed, and pushed the door shut behind me, assuming that Holmes would want to expand the reach of the dark lantern without it being observed by someone on the outside, in the unlikely chance there actually was someone else out on such a night at that lonely location.

As the light exposed the room, Holmes reached up and pushed back his fore-and-aft cap, allowing him to see around more clearly. It was a square chamber, as might be expected from observing the shape of the building from outside. There was only the one room, constructed of the same white marble, and quite plain. Along the walls were several raised platforms, or biers. Each of them was defined by ornate carvings along the top edges, and on the corners were mounted round marble balls about the size of my fist.

Only two of the biers were being used. Side by side on the left wall, near the rear of the room, were two plain coffins, the black wood of each held together at the corners by sturdy ironwork. Holmes stepped over and held the dark lantern this way and that. "I believe the village had a unique blacksmith earlier in the century. Whoever built the metal supports of these coffins certainly knew what he was about."

He leaned forward and wiped a thumb across the small brass plaques at the end of each coffin. Then, gesturing with the lantern toward the one farthest back in the corner, he said, "This one is that of Martin Briley's mother, and is nearly twenty years older than the other, that of Briley's father. Both have been here more than half-a-century, and still the unusual iron work has kept them in wonderful structural condition."

"Somehow," I replied softly, "I doubt that discovering this fact is what we are here for."

"You are correct," said Holmes. "Examination of this ornate metalwork only means that we are delayed for an extra moment or two longer than we would have been otherwise. The blacksmith of old has affixed cunning latches on each coffin, which I must understand before we can open them and view the occupants."

It was as I had expected, although I did not know what he hoped to accomplish. However, this was not the first time that I had found myself in this situation, and I was prepared to help in any way that I could.

Holmes succeeded in opening the rear coffin. Raising the lid, he lifted the dark lantern to a better vantage, as he simultaneously moved a step in order to give me easier access, so as to view the terrible contents.

It was as one might expect. She, or what was left of her, rested peacefully on the rotted linen remains which lined the box, wearing the gown in which she had been entombed. She was on her back, staring upward into eternity, the bones of her arms loosely folded across her breast. As unpleasant as the sight was, I saw nothing abnormal, and said as much to Holmes.

"As I expected," he replied. "But it pays to make certain. Performing this task once is enough, as I'm sure you will agree, and I wanted to make certain there was nothing unusual about the contents of this coffin, as well as the other one that we came to see."

He lowered the lid and returned the unusual latch to its closed position. Then, walking around to the other side of Galton Briley's coffin, he repeated his actions of a moment earlier and likewise raised that lid, uttering a small cry of satisfaction as he did so.

I stepped beside him, and could see that all was not as it should have been. The coffin contained the remains of a body, a figure taller than that of the woman's nearby. He was dressed in what was left of a suit of clothes of the style from over fifty years gone by. But, most unusually, the body was not lying flat on its back in the center of the coffin, staring upward as the woman's had been. Instead, it was rolled up onto its left side, facing the back wall of the coffin where the lid joined it by the long-ago blacksmith's hinges.

"Was this what you expected to find?" I asked.

"I wanted to confirm several things by the opening of this coffin. The shifting of the body answers one of my questions. Notice what is left of the linen lining underneath him."

"It appears to be pushed up against the man's back."

"Exactly. Even after all these years, it retains the flattening that occurred when something else was placed into the coffin beside Galton Briley's body. It would not have that appearance if the coffin had simply been tipped while being moved to the mausoleum or placed on the bier. At some point, this coffin was opened, the body was pushed up and rolled aside toward the back wall, and something was jammed in here for some amount of time, long enough to flatten the lining."

"Something like the body of the man found under the pipe?" I asked. "Are you suggesting that before the murdered man was placed under the pipe, he was put in this coffin for a time, long enough to have made an impression on the lining?"

"That is exactly what I believe happened. After the man was murdered, he was stored here until he could be moved to the trench excavation, where it was believed he would remain undiscovered forever."

"And is *this* what you hoped to discover?"

"Not specifically. What I wanted to absolutely ascertain first was whether this was actually Galton Briley in this coffin, and that he was *not* the body that was found in the trench."

"But we decided that the man found under the pipe was clearly younger. Galton Briley was an old man when he died."

"We did agree that the body was that of a young man, but we could not be absolutely certain based simply upon our limited examination, and also because of the mummified man's condition. The peat-like fluids that had leached into the body had darkened and wrinkled the skin, and leathered it.

Also, what remained of the mummy's hair might have absorbed some of the tannic acid in the peat, giving us a false idea of a darker and younger color. No, an examination of this man's body, who had died at the same approximate time as that of the man in the trench, had to be done. Otherwise, there would still have been an element of uncertainty.

"But there is one other factor to consider, while we have the chance. This man's right hand, Watson. Look at his right hand."

Leaning past him at an awkward angle, I put my head closer, even as he moved the dark lantern to a more advantageous location. As the body had been rolled up to face the rear of the coffin, the right hand had dropped behind it, resting on the wrinkled linens. Of course, the flesh was gone, or what was left of it was too insignificant to recognize in the unnatural light of the lantern. But the bones were there. They had collapsed, but were lying neatly on the cloth. A quick examination and count confirmed that the body was a Briley.

"There are no little finger bones from this hand. I count twenty-four of the twenty-seven bones that should be here. There are no distal, intermediate, or proximal phalanges of the correct size, and at the metacarpophalangeal joint where the little finger would normally be attached, the end of the metacarpal bone is strangely deformed. It appears to be a natural deformity, and not due to some injury, I think that we are seeing the characteristic missing Briley finger, and we may conclude that this man was, in fact, Galton Briley."

"Very satisfactory, Watson," said Holmes. "Now, I think we can close this fellow up and let him return to his rest."

"But, Holmes," I said, "shouldn't we examine the remains while we have the chance, to see if there is any evidence that Galton Briley was also murdered? After all, we may not have this opportunity again."

"I think not. If he were poisoned, there would be no way to know it at this point without further tests, and if he were stabbed, the only possibility of determining it is by a careful examination of the remaining bones, on the chance that the knife had possibly nicked one as it entered the body. As you can see, the skull seems to be intact, so there is no indication that this man died from a head wound, as did the man in the trench. No, Watson. Even if Galton Briley was murdered, it is incidental to our investigation. And there is every chance that if we discover the truth about the death of the man in the trench, a death that we believe to have been a murder, then any crime that might possibly be related to this man will most likely also be revealed."

"Should we . . . turn him onto his back? As he undoubtedly was before he was pushed up into this position by whoever stored the other body here?"

Holmes shook his head. "Let us leave him as we found him, facing his wife. There is no indignity in that, I think, at this late date."

Holmes closed the lid and latched it. Stepping back, Holmes looked at the coffin for a moment, and then ran his hands along it. At the foot, he let them drop onto one of the decorative marble balls on the corner of the bier. It rolled loosely in his grip, and he took it off.

He bent to examine the corner where it had rested for so many years. There was some type of grout or mortar there, long dried, cupped in a shape to match the ball in Holmes's hand. He hefted it for a time or two, and then made a swinging motion with it, at about eye level. Then he nodded and turned to me.

"I believe this might be the murder weapon, my friend," he said, handing it to me. I also examined it, guessing it to be about ten or twelve pounds. I ran my hand around its cold smoothness.

"It is certainly the right size," I said. "Was this also something that you expected to find here?"

"Not at all," he replied, "but it does not raise any objections to my theoretical construct of the events of long ago."

"Why was he not left here?"

"There was always the possibility that the coffin might have been reopened, especially if someone came to question the odd events surrounding the death and burial of Galton Briley."

"But," I asked, "isn't it possible that the man in the trench died by accident? Couldn't he have fallen against the marble fixture? Stranger things have happened."

"Not likely, I think. Why else was so much trouble taken to hide him, in two different places? The logical conclusion is that he was murdered.

"In fact, I can imagine how it must have happened. The murdered man was lured here, where he was killed, and then immediately put into Galton Briley's coffin. It would have been easier to get the victim to come here himself, rather than trying to move a body here after the fact. What could have been more convenient for our murderer?

"What indeed," I said softly, replacing the marble ball back on its resting place.

Then, looking around for just a moment or two more in order to make sure that there was nothing else to be seen in the bare chamber, we turned and departed, narrowing the dark lantern's aperture nearly shut as we reached the door. Within minutes, we had departed, and the door was relocked as before.

"Well, Watson," said Holmes, as we both breathed deeply of the damp cool air as we stood on the porch. "We have a long uphill trek through darkness and rain back to the house. And then I believe that we might as well see an end to this matter. Are you game?"

"Yes," I said. "Let us have done with this," I said, and we set off.

The journey back was unpleasant, as might be imagined. The thunder still crashed intermittently in the distance, and the rain, which had been falling in straight, icy sheets, was now being whipped by the winds as the latest portion of the storm approached. It did not help that we were now climbing the hill while facing into the saturated breezes. When we finally reached a point on the hill close enough to see the house, I nearly gave a weak cheer. But I did not, because our desire was to return to the house in as discreet a manner as we had left it, and also because I could not have found the breath to do so in any case.

The house was in much the same condition as when we had departed, with one difference. Where before there had been two rooms with lights burning on the left rear side facing the back of the structure, now there was only one. The upper story window, which we understood to be that of Mrs. Lynch's room, was now dark. Only the ground floor room containing Martin Briley was still lit. The view of it had suddenly ruined my night vision, and all I could see now was the light spilling down the hill toward us. I looked down and could not even see my hands.

Holmes resumed the uphill trudge, but instead of turning toward the right, and the stairs that we had earlier used to exit the house, he angled to the left, and the brightly lit room. "Do you intend to have an immediate confrontation?" I asked.

"Yes," he replied. "Unless you would rather find dry clothing first."

I sighed. "Not at all. Let us continue. But did you not tell Mrs. Lynch that you had no further need to speak to Mr. Briley?"

"That is exactly correct," he replied, "I do not." He added nothing further.

We found the steps leading to the landing outside the door of Briley's room. Crossing the stones, Holmes led me to the door, and then paused. I stood beside him, feeling warm underneath my coat despite the damp and the rain. My shoes, of course, were soaked, but hopefully I would be able to do something about that sooner rather than later.

Holmes reached out for the handle of the door, and gently turned it. It moved freely and silently. Without opening the door, he murmured to me, "It seems that we are expected." Then, pushing the door open, he stepped in, and I followed.

A voice spoke to us, one that I recognized. "Come in, gentlemen, and warm yourself. It is a most terrible night to be out."

Chapter 11 – The Unqualified Truth

Martin Briley was standing near the fireplace, looking more hearty than he had appeared several hours ago, when he was ensconced in his special bath chair by the fire. It was pushed off to the side now, piled with the blankets that had covered him from head to foot. He was beside one of a pair of fine chairs, between us and the fireplace. He was wrapped tightly in an expensive dressing gown, with his hands folded neatly in front of him.

I could see I had been right earlier, when I decided that he had, at some time in the past, been a much stronger physical figure than the one that now presented itself. His clothing, while well made, seemed to hang from him. The cut of his dressing gown across his shoulders appeared to be just a shade too wide, allowing the seams to sag where they would have been supported in years past by muscle. Earlier in the day, he had appeared to be near death's door. Now, he still had that door in sight, but he wasn't quite through it yet.

Beside him, on a small table between the two chairs, was a green book, shut with what appeared to be two envelopes protruding from the top edge. Next to it was a small bottle containing some warm-looking amber liquid and two snifters. A coal fire burned in the hearth, and I was very grateful for it indeed, as it had warmed the room to the point that it might have seemed uncomfortable after a long period, while just now it felt wonderful.

The portrait of Galton Briley still hung on the wall, of course, but its colors seemed darker and more melancholy without the little bit of daylight that had illuminated it earlier. I looked at it for a few seconds, trying to reconcile the hearty man painted in his forties, as he had been portrayed by the artist at the turn of the century, with those sad and disrupted remains that Holmes and I had examined less than a half-hour before.

The old man stepped back, and sank into the chair on his left, watching us as we approached. He smiled warmly, and I was reminded of all the good works that he had done in this part of the world through the long years. What set of circumstances could have occurred so ago that would have entangled such a benevolent fellow as this?

The rain rattled against the door and windows, and soon another round of thunder followed. I was conscious that my wet shoes were tracking moisture across the fine rugs lining the floor, but there was nothing to do about it now.

"I was expecting you," he said. "I left the door to the terrace unlocked, along with the one to the hall, should you have wished to approach from either side. I suspected you might have something to ask that you didn't before. Possibly some questions to be discussed in confidence."

"Perhaps one or two," said Holmes. "Simply to clarify certain events. However, I believe that we have already been able to piece together enough of an idea of what has remained hidden for so long."

Briley nodded, watching from beneath lowered brows. His gaze was intent, but I perceived no menace from him. Slowly, he unfolded his hands in his lap. "Earlier today, Mr. Holmes, you asked if you could shake my hand. At the time I refused. It was then I realized for certain that you knew some, if not all, of the truth. My composure was quite shaken, and I reacted badly. Refusing to shake hands then has only delayed the inevitable, although it did give me a chance to arrange some things on my own terms. But now I am ready." He held out his right hand. "Mr. Holmes, do you still wish to shake my hand?"

Holmes smiled and looked at him for a moment. Then, without raising his own, he stepped slightly to the side, where he could get a better view of Briley's outstretched right hand. Briley, appearing to be puzzled, did not lower it as the awkward moment lengthened. Holmes then leaned in, looked closely, nodded once, and straightened.

"Perhaps some other time. But would you mind if, instead of shaking hands with me, that Dr. Watson had the honor?" He turned his head in my direction.

Puzzled, but finding no objection, I moved to Briley's side. Raising my own hand, I wondered what Holmes was hoping to accomplish by this unusual action. Briley, with a resigned look, as if he were crossing some personal Rubicon, reached out in my direction and clasped his hand to mine with the strength of a much younger man.

We held the grip for a second, and then I realized what it was that Holmes wanted me to find. A look of enlightened understanding must have passed across my face. Easing my hold on Briley's hand, I shifted my own fingers so as to hold his palm in the manner of a doctor examining a patient. Turning his hand onto its side, I leaned down and examined the outer edge.

"Holmes," I said. "There is a scar! A scar where the little finger should be!"

Briley pulled his hand away, not in a sudden and angry way, but simply as if he was tired of holding it up. He returned it to his lap, where he folded his left hand around it in a protective way.

I straightened up. "It is an old scar, with no obvious discoloration, at least that I can identify in this light. But there is a definite raised ridge of scarred tissue there." I turned away from Briley, whom I had been watching as I spoke. He continued to look toward Holmes. "Could it be a scar from some unrelated wound? At the site of the missing Briley little finger? Or did he — ?"

"Is that the confirmation that you needed, Mr. Holmes?" Briley asked, ignoring me completely.

"Yes, it is . . . Mr. Lynch."

Lynch! The name seemed to hang in the quiet room. Suddenly I began to have a better understanding of what must have taken place, those many years ago. But there was too much that was still unexplained, at least to me. And I had no idea what path Holmes had followed to reach his solution. He had referred to a similar case thirty or more years earlier in Nimes, but had that been enough to reveal the truth to him? Apparently Martin Briley, or rather, the man whom I had thought to *be* Martin Briley, was as puzzled as I was.

"I . . . I had come to believe that you knew the truth about the identity of the man found beneath the pipe, Mr. Holmes. But I was just as certain that you did *not* know the whole story. I was prepared to tell the entire tale, but I thought that parts of it would surprise you, including who I really am. Instead, you call me by a name that I have not used since 1840, revealing that you truly *do* know everything."

"Not quite," said Holmes. He pulled off his fore-and-aft, ran his long thin fingers through his hair, and began to divest himself of his wet Inverness. He looked around for an appropriate location to place it, but seeing nowhere to lay it except across the room's fine furniture, he finally deposited it carefully on the floor opposite the fireplace, near the door. Realizing that the room was becoming quite warm, and surprised at myself that I would find it to be so after being so cold and miserable just moments before, I removed my coat and hat as well. I placed them by Holmes's, as Briley — that is, Lynch — continued speaking.

"But how did you know?" he asked. "Of my true name, I mean."

"By the observation of your ears."

"My ears?" repeated Lynch.

"Yes. They have the unique characteristic of being small, and of having the outer rim, or *auricle*, shaped in something of a compression. It can be a family trait. I had happened to notice Mrs. Lynch's ears earlier today, when we were first introduced to her, and I observed the formation of her ears at that time. I had happened to be thinking of ears a littler earlier in the afternoon, as I will explain in a moment. Later, when we were brought in here to speak to you, I found that your ears presented the same shape. There is no doubt that *she* is the person that she has always claimed to be, Elizabeth Lynch. This is confirmed by the testimony of an old man in the village, who has known her for her whole life. Therefore, if you have the Lynch ear, and you are *not* a Briley, it follows that you must be a Lynch."

"But . . . this is incredible, Mr. Holmes," said Lynch.

Holmes ignored him, and instead took a step to the side, gesturing toward the painting of Galton Briley, hanging on the wall. "Furthermore, having noticed the similarity between your ears and those of Mrs. Lynch, and thus confirming that this inherited family characteristic indicated a blood relation between you and her, I next wanted to satisfy my doubts regarding your legitimacy as the true heir to the Briley family. We were fortunate enough to find Galton Briley's portrait, making the job quite a bit easier. Examining the right ear shown on the painting's subject indicated to me that, along with not sharing the characteristic Briley finger, which I did not know at the time, you also do not have the Briley ear."

I stepped to the painting and saw that he was correct. The careful representation, so accurate in detail from fingernails to eyebrows, also presented a clear image of the right side of Galton Briley's face. The figure was turned into a three-quarter view, so that his right hand, with its missing finger, presented itself, along with the man's right ear. It was not a small ear at all, and looked nothing like that of the man seated nearby. Rather, the rim was flared, and once noticed, could not be ignored.

"But Holmes," I asked. "How do you know that this ear in the painting is a characteristic of the Briley family? It might simply be that Galton Briley's ear had that particular shape, with no correspondence to the ears of any his other relations."

"I know that it is another shared characteristic of the Brileys, because we have seen another such ear much like it elsewhere today," he replied.

I thought for a moment. "Someone in the village?" I asked.

"No, Watson. We have seen a very similar ear on the body of the man found in the trench. Though it was quite mummified, his ear still retains the same shape as that shown in the painting. I noticed how well it was preserved when we examined the body, but gave it no more thought at the time, simply cataloging my observations as a part of my general examination. It was merely a curiosity.

"Later, when we were introduced to Mr. Lynch here, in his guise as the Briley heir, I compared his ear to my recollection of the dead man's. Obviously, they did not match. We had already decided that the man in the trench was a Briley, based on the fact that his missing finger seemed to have occurred naturally, with no signs of a corresponding injury. This knowledge was augmented when I saw that the ear in the painting of a genuine Briley *did* match that of the dead man. When I had an opportunity to observe Mr. Lynch's ear, it did not match *either* of the Briley ears.

"In any case, by the time we were allowed to interview Mr. Lynch, I already had some hint as to the identity of both the dead man and Mr. Lynch."

"And may I ask how, Mr. Holmes?" said Lynch.

"Certainly. My knowledge of past crimes is extensive, and it has often been of some use to me. I must admit I was aware of a matter with many similarities to this one that took place decades ago, in France. There was a family much like the Brileys, with a widowed father and an estranged son. When the old man died, an imposter took the place of the heir. Years later, the true son's body was found, and all was revealed.

"While I do not yet know the specifics of how events in *this* location played out, all those years ago, I feel certain that the unfortunate dead man in the trench is not some illegitimate child of Galton Briley, as Watson has theorized, or perhaps an unknown cousin. Rather, he is in fact *Martin Briley, the true and actual heir*, who was murdered and hidden upon his return to the village at the time of his father's death. At that point, you, with the connivance of your sister, took his place, and have held it to this day."

"His sister?" I said. "Then Mrs. Lynch is his sister?"

"Exactly. I do not know how she came to her position as housekeeper under old Galton Briley, while still very young, and the squalid disagreeable details are probably unimportant at this late date. However, when the old man died, and it was time for his son Martin to return from London, his murder was arranged. Mr. Lynch, here, who had also moved away long before, returned and took Martin's place. Does that cover the basic facts, Mr. Lynch?"

"Yes." He swallowed, and repeated, "Yes, it does. But there are aspects of the matter that you do not yet know. And I will explain them to you. But first, tell me how you knew these things before you even entered this room? I could tell that you suspected the truth when you came in here, before I refused to shake your hand. Comparing my ear to that of Galton Briley in the painting was only an afterthought. How did you come to discover that Elizabeth is my sister? I have heard of your reputation before you ever walked through our door, but I still want to hear how you knew!"

"Today in the village," replied Holmes, "I spoke at length with an old man, formerly of the stables, named Abner." Lynch nodded in recognition, and Holmes continued. "As he told me, he is probably the only person left within miles who is old enough to remember the long-ago days when Mrs. Lynch, then known as *Miss* Lynch, or simply Elizabeth, came to work in the house. One of the other facts that he mentioned in passing was that she had come from a poor family, always barely scrabbling by, and often living on charity due to the actions of her shiftless father."

Lynch winced at this statement, but Holmes continued. "One thing that Abner mentioned was that young Elizabeth Lynch had been the older of two children, the younger being a brother, who had fled the area while still in his teens after a particularly brutal beating by the siblings' father, during one of his many drunken episodes. Abner seemed to attach no more significance to this event.

"On the way back to the house from the village, I paused at the church to examine the parish records and confirmed the existence of this brother, one Peter Lynch, born in 1821. That would be you, would it not, Mr. Lynch?"

Lynch simply nodded, and then closed his eyes. "It has been most of my life since I last saw my brute of a father, and still the memory of him affects me, as you can see."

Holmes nodded. "Further confirmation of your relation to Mrs. Lynch came when we were introduced late this afternoon. At the same time I became aware that you did not have the Briley ear, I saw that you *did* possess the same ear type as Mrs. Lynch, which I had already chanced to particularly notice earlier in the day."

Lynch pondered this for a moment, and then seized on an aspect of Holmes's statement. "But why had you noticed my sister's ear before that?"

"Because, I had seen a very similar ear earlier this afternoon, before we were even introduced to Mrs. Lynch."

I had caught up by that point, and I blurted, "Burton! George Burton has that type of ear!"

"Very good, Watson! Very good, indeed! When we examined the mummified body in the cottage, I remarked to myself on the exceptionally well-preserved condition of the ear, along with the rest of the fellow. With ears still on my mind, I idly glanced at other ears as we began our journey back to the house, and in doing so, I cataloged Burton's ear type, comparing it to MacDonald's and Watson's, both of whose I had observed and classified years ago. Then I thought no more about it until we reached the house. I confess that I was astonished to see that Mrs. Lynch had the same type of ear as Burton's. They were obviously related, but I saw no indication of any acknowledgement of the fact between them. In truth, they seemed to be warily hostile of one another.

"Then, when Burton told us the story of his adoption into the household, I began to piece together a possible connection to you, Mr. Lynch. After all, it seemed unlikely that you would adopt a village orphan to be your apparent heir for no obvious reason. It was far more likely that there was some hidden relation between the two of you, however unknown. It only took an observation of your own ears, showing the same family characteristic, to confirm it. George Burton is also a Lynch."

In spite of the number of times I had been exposed to Holmes's gifts, I could not suppress a soft, "Amazing."

"Not at all, Watson," said Holmes. "As I told you, by that time you had seen all that I had seen, the ears of both the living and the dead. Abner's story simply filled in confirming details. The family traits had been observable before that conversation. However," he added charitably, "I am sure that you would have eventually reached the same conclusion yourself, having now been exposed to my methods for so long."

I was pleased by Holmes's faith in me, but I doubted that his belief that I would have puzzled it out would actually have come to fruition. A thought occurred to me. "Mrs. Lynch is unlikely to be Burton's mother, as there is no indication that she has ever had a child. Therefore, that means that – "

"Yes, doctor. It means that I am George Burton's father," said Lynch quietly. "His mother was a new widow when we met, and it was true love between us, although she would not let me acknowledge it. She felt ashamed of us. She pretended that the boy was the child of her recently deceased husband, although we both knew differently, and the villagers believed her. I managed to find a way to get money to them as George grew. And then she died, and I was able to take him in, although I never revealed the truth, as doing so would destroy my beloved's reputation, along with the love the boy felt for his dead mother."

"The conclusion that Burton is your son was quite easy to theorize," said Holmes, "considering how Burton was brought here after the death of his mother for no apparent reason, in your guise of Martin Briley, and trained to one day take over the estate."

"But not legitimately," I stated. "After all, it is *not* actually this man's estate to pass on." I gestured toward Lynch. "It does not matter whether or not Burton is Lynch's heir, or that Burton has been trained since childhood to run the place. Neither is a Briley. The estate should go to the true heirs of the Briley family."

"My research in the parish records suggested that there are no true heirs, Watson. And Abner believes that there were no illegitimate ones, either. He is certain that such a thing would have been a well known fact in those days. Just to make certain, I have MacDonald in London tracking down the last verification. But in any case, I'm sure that the Briley line died out with the true Martin Briley, forty-eight years ago."

"And so this man has gotten away with murder for half a century!" I cried.

"In his case, Watson, I feel safe to say that the accurate description of the situation is that he has gotten away with *covering up a murder*, since he did not commit the actual crime itself. Am I also right about that, Mr. Lynch?"

Lynch nodded. "I see that you understand everything. But how do you know that? Did Abner suspect something for all these years? Did we leave some clue, perhaps on the body, unseen at the time but obvious under your examination, that told you the whole story?"

"It was simply a matter of the timing. From what I understand, your sister had lived in the house for several years up to the time of Galton Briley's death. She was conniving enough to have made herself the housekeeper while still nearly a girl. I believe that it was her planning behind all of this. I don't think that you, living away from here in the years leading up to old Galton Briley's death, could have adequately contrived such an event from a distance.

"However, your sister *was* living in the house, knowledgeable at each hour of how Galton Briley was sinking, and aware that Martin Briley was being called home, returning after several years as a near stranger to his father and the village. Finally, she was the kind of sister who, according to Abner, had always tried to protect her younger brother. This protection extended to the point of killing in order to allow her brother to assume a life of luxury."

"Mrs. Lynch," I breathed. "She was the murderer."

"Yes," said Lynch. "It was my sister who did the deed." He shifted in the chair, and then he began to cough, a racking, deep cough that seemed to tear at him from inside out. His face reddened, and tears fell involuntarily from his clenched eyes. I had nearly forgotten that he was as ill as all that, as we had found him standing when we arrived, and out of his sick chair.

I rushed to his side and supported him while the coughing eased. As he sat back and caught his breath, I turned to the small table beside him, took the stopper from the oddly shaped bottle containing the amber liquid, and poured a finger or two into the glass snifter beside it. Handing it to him, I said, "Here, drink this. It will help."

"Thank you, doctor," he said, straightening up and adjusting his dressing gown. "Your kindness toward an old man is much appreciated." He held the glass in his right hand, but did not drink.

"You are correct in your suppositions, Mr. Holmes," he said. "I knew when George told me that the Inspector was bringing you here, time was probably starting to run out.

"I believe," he said, "that you should know the true story of what happened in the spring of 1840, when Galton Briley's iron constitution began to fail, and my sister saw a way to not only preserve her position within the household, but also to find a place for her baby brother, back here in the village of his birth, instead of surrounded by the terrible dangers of London. Sometimes I wish I had never answered her summons!" He shook his head. "What might have been, but for the formation of that first link on that one memorable day?"

Chapter 12 – The Old Man's Tale

As the storm grew outside, Lynch tried to make himself more comfortable. He shifted in his chair, and gently set the glass back on the small table beside him, untouched. Then the old man began his tale. The thunder increased as the rain lashed at the windows, but we did not hear it, as we were drawn back into those long ago days before either Holmes or I were born.

"I'm from this village," began Lynch, "born not a mile from where we are now. And you cannot imagine a more different set of circumstances. It was in a little house there, and it still stands, although many were the times when I was younger, after I had obtained the money and influence that came from the Briley estate, that I thought about having it knocked down. Instead, I made sure it was one of the best-kept homes around, and that the children living there never had to go through what I did. Pray to God no child ever should, but I know that they will. Even with access to the Briley fortune, there was only so much I could do.

"As you said, Mr. Holmes, I was born in 1821, a year after the true Martin Briley. My father brought my mother and my sister here before I was born. My sister was very young then. My father had been employed by the East India company in his youth, but he would never speak of it, save with a bitter jibe or a sneer, so we learned not to bring the subject up. Therefore, I never learned much else about my antecedents. I have no knowledge of where my father met my mother, or where she came from. And having discussed it with my sister when we were younger, I know that she is as ignorant as I am.

"In any case, here my father brought his family, and here I was born. He worked as a hand in the fields, but somehow he was knowledgeable enough about things that mattered that he was given a position of greater responsibility, and thus a small house. In those days, Galton Briley managed things quite differently than I have, and the houses at times were little better than wind-breaks with poorly fitted roofs. I recall many a night when it seemed that the inside of our little house was colder than the outside, as the cracks and crannies seemed to focus the wind into a living thing with a vengeance against me.

"My father must have been a successful man at some time in the past, because he was always well spoken, and never crude. Sadly, it was this ability which allowed him to aim his bitter tongue at each member of his family with the accuracy of an Italian *stiletto*. And when he was drinking, matters became so much worse. As time went on, he drank more and more. No doubt it is a story you've heard many times before, but it is where mine begins, and where I started on the long road to end up here, tonight.

"I know that you gentlemen don't want to hear a list of every one of my father's torments upon his own family, and it's not relevant to our discussion. Suffice it to say, as time went on, my mother weakened, and was less and less able to defend her children. My father tended to save special attention to me, as I was the boy, and he seemed to expect something from me that I was not able to provide. It fell to my sister, nine years my senior, to defend and shield me when my mother could not. She did the best that she could, but it could not help but to transform her into the hard, cold, and mistrustful woman she is today. The kind of woman who would have no hesitation about taking what she felt that she deserved, and being quite ruthless about it.

"When I was about fourteen, my mother died, leaving us with only our father for a parent. He had become even more unpleasant as the years and the drink affected him. At that time, I was already finding work in the village, as old Mr. Briley certainly did not provide any schools for the local children. My sister had already gone to work in this very house, and as such no longer lived at home. It was just me and my father in the little house now, and he turned his full bitterness upon me.

"My sister was worried more than she would ever admit, and a few months after our mother died, she finally urged me to be away from here, rather than take anything else off of my father. I believe she was also worried that, as I reached my full growth, I would some day turn on my father and in anger do something which I would either regret, which wasn't likely, or perhaps commit some act against him that would lead to my arrest. I must admit, when she explained I would need to leave and break ties from this area completely, I was greatly intrigued by the idea. We both knew that if I stayed, I would never be completely free of my father. I decided I would go to London.

"As I said, I believe my father must have been a successful man at some time in the past. He was also an educated man, and in spite of my many grievances against him, I must be thankful that he saw to it that I learned to read. This allowed me to find my way to other areas of learning, and I soon taught myself enough to know how much I did *not* know. I have pursued knowledge from the time that I was small, and when I went to London, I managed to find a place in a school, perhaps the best place I could have landed at the time.

"Of course, I was not a student. Rather, I was a young man of all work. But I did manage to teach myself the basics of mathematics, and also get my first exposure to literature and philosophy, reading books that were left unused and unopened by the students. The owners of the school were good, kind-hearted people, nothing like characters that might be portrayed in a Dickens novel. I was very satisfied, and believed that staying there would comprise the rest of my life. At that age, I had no true idea about how long a life can really be. And then, after I had lived there for several years, my sister wrote to say that Mr. Galton Briley's death was imminent, and that I needed to hurry home immediately.

"I had no idea why I should be present for such an event. I had only seen old Mr. Briley in the village on a handful of occasions, and had certainly never actually met him. His death would mean nothing to me. Yet, my sister urged me to come home, and how could I refuse her?

"We had remained in touch during the years I was up to London. We wrote on a regular basis, and she was always very encouraging when I would describe the things I was learning, or relate some of the added responsibilities I was taking on at the school. She had always sent money, and over time the amounts increased. Long before she had been elevated from her earlier position to that of head housekeeper, but I understood that the less I knew about her methods, the better.

"So having decided to obey my sister's command, I traveled back here from London. It was raining when I arrived in the village. This was before there were trains. I had ridden in coaches all day, and found it very wearying. My sister had given me specific instructions about which routes and times I should travel. I learned later that this was intentional, as my traveling companion was also someone who was returning to this village after a long time away. He had made his plans known to my sister in her position as the housekeeper, thus allowing her to be certain that I would be journeying with him. Of course, I'm referring to Martin Briley, coming home for the impending death of his father.

"Martin was a year older than I was, and had also left for London following a disagreement with *his* father, although it was a year or so before I departed. By that time, we had both been gone for a number of years. Quite frankly, I did not recognize him as we rode the coaches, as he had changed considerably, and as he was more drunk than not throughout the entire day. There was no conversation between us that would have provided any opportunity to realize that we had this village in common. When we eventually reached the village, we were traveling by ourselves.

"We were met at the inn by my sister, who was driving a carriage. She had always been strong and independent, and did not worry at all about anyone's opinion of her. I would guess that people might have thought it unusual for a woman to be driving in that day and age. They still do now sometimes, I suppose. But when I saw her there, I was not surprised at all.

"She nodded to me in her reserved way, for she has never been an affectionate person, and then spoke to Martin Briley, telling him that the carriage was ready for him. She rushed him into it before anyone took notice of us. Martin climbed in, without seeming to give it any thought when she ascended to the driver's bench. I joined her there, and I don't think Martin even realized that the same man who had been traveling with him all day was going on with him to his family's estate.

"I wanted to ask my sister why she had summoned me, and I also wanted to ascertain what the chances were that we might encounter my father. But I held my tongue, not wanting to have any conversation in front of Martin, although it was doubtful that he would have cared anyway, as he seemed to have finally passed out from his day of drinking.

"As we drove onto the estate, my sister took the side road that runs down and behind the house, rather than along the main road leading past the front door, and then so on to the cottages. Again, I wanted to ask her questions, but I refrained, trusting her as I always had. Even when she brought the horse to a stop at the Briley mausoleum, overlooking the stream and the fields beyond, I kept my thoughts to myself.

"My sister climbed down and went to the side of the carriage. She reached inside and shook Briley until he awoke. 'We're here,' she said. 'I knew you'd want to see your father as soon as you could.' I thought I understood why we had come to the mausoleum, to see the dead body of Galton Briley, but I believed my sister's handling of the situation seemed to be in very poor taste, and was unnecessarily cruel to Martin Briley, no matter what sort of wastrel he seemed to have turned out to be.

"As he dropped to the ground, Briley seemed to wake up, but he still staggered with every step as my sister led him to the mausoleum door. The building was much newer then, of course, as it had only been built when Galton Briley's wife was slowly approaching her death. They say he loved his wife, as cold as he was. When she was ill, he built the mausoleum to honor her, and when she died, he had a matching coffin built for himself to lie beside her.

"We reached the mausoleum door, which was unlocked, and my sister pushed it open and led Martin inside. I followed, dreading what I thought was about to happen, and having no idea what my sister had actually planned.

"For I had believed that she simply intended to lead Martin to his father's coffin as a way of letting him know that the old man had died. I had thought it heartless, but I did not intervene. Even as we stepped closer to the coffin, with its lid open, I could not stop myself from following. The chamber was lit by several lanterns, and the hellish yellows and reds from the flames, as reflected by the cold marble walls, sent a thrill of terror through me. I did not want to see what was in that coffin, and yet I could not turn away.

"My sister led Martin Briley right to the side of the ornate box, and then left him, stepping away for just a moment. I moved closer, and was just able to see the ghastly form of Galton Briley lying there, when Martin opened his mouth, the beginnings of a wail on his lips, as the full realization fell upon him. It was at that moment that my sister pushed me roughly aside. She stepped behind Martin Briley, and swung her arm into his head. I could see that she held a round object, which I later learned was a decorative marble fixture from the tomb. Briley's cry stopped abruptly, and he sank to the floor, a horrible soft moan leaking from his dying lungs.

"I was aghast at what my sister had done. She stood looking at Martin for a moment, before straightening herself with a determined shake and replacing the marble fixture. And then she turned to me and spoke.

" 'I have always tried to protect you, and to make a better life for you. This you know to be true. And even now, you must trust me. I will tell you this. I have had to sacrifice much to achieve the position I now hold, and I will never speak —

even to you! — of what I have had to do. But you must understand that Galton Briley was an evil man. An *evil* man! I have *known* his evil. And before he departed for London, Martin Briley, the son, was evil as well. I have managed to stay informed, through his father, of Martin's rakish and wanton life, and he was not fit to live, anymore than his father. That is all I will tell you. You must trust me. But for now, help me get him into the coffin with his accursed father.'

"I know how the body of Martin Briley was found by the workmen under the pipe a few days ago. That was where it was eventually hidden, some days later, with the belief that it would never be found. But initially, we put the body into the coffin of Galton Briley. The old man had died a few days before my return to the village, and the funeral — such as it was — had already been conducted. My sister had managed everything, including what information was given out relating to the return of Martin Briley. She had told everyone who cared, and I'm sure that there were very few, that she had sent for him, but he was not going to be able to make it back home in time to see his father laid to rest. However, he would be expected at some unknown point in the future, to claim his inheritance.

"She had also sent a message to Martin Briley, telling him that his father was only sick, and not yet dead. She made the specific arrangements for his travels so that she would know exactly when he was entering her web. Such was the fear of her around the estate, even then, that she had no problem at all fixing things exactly as she wanted them. For she had conceived a plan, a bold plan indeed, and she meant to bring it to fruition.

"And so we concealed Martin's body in the coffin. Before that, however, my sister had me change clothes with him, so I would be wearing those of the dead man. I was moving as if in a fog, still shocked by my sister's actions, and willing to trust her as she had asked, but her request did not make sense to me at first. Later, I learned that she wanted to make sure that if I were unexpectedly seen after we left the mausoleum, I would be mistakenly recognized by my better clothing as the wealthy heir. But that was beyond my understanding in that moment. All I knew then was that my sister had committed a murder, and I was wearing a dead man's clothing that was too big for me.

"After wrestling Martin into my clothes, we lifted him up and rolled him into the coffin, holding up his father's body to make room. To this day, I'm not certain if my sister's blow actually killed Martin Briley immediately, or if he died later, sealed in his father's coffin, shoved up against his father's corpse.

"After we put the body into the coffin and shut the lid, my sister pulled me down beside her on one of the empty platforms, built for nonexistent members of the Briley family that would now never occupy them. The line was extinct. Even then, we knew that. It had always been common knowledge that Galton Briley had no living relatives, near or distant, except for his son. There were no heirs. And so, my sister explained, she had decided to make *me the heir!*

"She laid it all out quite succinctly. No one in the village had seen me in a number of years, and in the meantime I had grown and filled out. I did not look anything like the boy that I had been. I walked upright with a certain amount of pride now, reflecting the inner man I had constructed. No one would recognize me. And most of all, our father was dead, and he could certainly never tell anyone that I had returned.

"I was surprised at the death of my father, and more than a little suspicious about it, but my sister explained without emotion that he had passed not long after my departure, and she did not want to burden me, far away in London, with any thoughts wasted in his direction. After my initial surprise, I realized she was correct. I was better off without him in every respect.

"But I asked her, how would I fool everyone into thinking that I was Martin Briley, the long lost prodigal son? My sister had also considered that. She believed he had been gone long enough so that few would remember him very clearly. The household staff had completely changed by this point, never lasting too long in the presence of both Galton Briley and my sister. As an adult, I now superficially resembled Martin Briley, enough to fool anyone who might need to have dealings with me. There was only one thing that needed to be done, in order to carry off the impersonation . . . .

"My sister has always been a hard woman, and she needed to be, in order to do what must be done. In many ways, I was the weak one. I've long suspected, although she kept her word and never discussed it, that old Galton Briley was carried off before his time. I even believe, deep down, that my sister visited her form of justice upon our father. And she knew what had to be done to finish changing me into Martin Briley. I never would have been able to face it on my own. My sister gave me the strength and the courage. The last thing we did that night, in the hellish light of the mausoleum, was to complete the transformation.

"In her preparations for Martin Briley's arrival, my sister had also brought some other necessary supplies with her to the mausoleum. Holding my gaze, giving me strength to do what we had to do, she laid my hand across the empty platform where we sat, resting it upon clean linens, as we had tried to make the conditions there as clean as possible. I bit down on a wooden dowel, wrapped in rags, and closed my eyes. The last thing I saw, before the incredible pain took me, was my sister raising the hatchet, already looking bloody in the reddish lantern light, over my extended little finger."

He paused for a moment, swallowing once or twice with the memory, still fresh after these many years. I shook my head, as if to chase away the dreadful picture that he had painted. I glanced over at Holmes, who was staring intently at our host, his pipe clenched in his teeth. I realized that I had been completely unaware that he had lit it.

"While I was unconscious," continued Lynch, "my sister poured whisky liberally over the wound, making sure that it came into contact with all the raw and affected areas. Beforehand, she had also poured it over the hatchet blade. By the time I was coming around, she was nearly finished bandaging my hand.

"The pain was unbearable, but somehow I made it back to the carriage, which she drove back to the house. No one saw us, as had been planned and arranged by my sister. She got me inside, and put me to bed in Galton Briley's room. And for the next three weeks, she nursed me, scouring out the infection that tried to take root in my hand, and helping me through the fever. She had told the staff that Martin Briley had returned, but was in a state of near death from his debauched London lifestyle. She was helping me to recover, so that I could take over the running of the estate.

"During the weeks that I was in bed, there had only been one visitor, the old man who was Galton Briley's attorney and man of business. It seems that he had never known Martin Briley very well at all, but did know about his reputation. It was no surprise to him that I was recovering in bed all that time. Later, when I was able to get up and about, I met with him in this very room, bundled up much as you found me today, feigning that I had a chill and could not shake his hand. He believed it all, and happily entrusted me with the care and keeping of Galton Briley's fortune, which turned out to be sizably more than either I or my sister had believed.

"Sometime during my recovery, Elizabeth went alone to the mausoleum, and moved the body to what was supposed to be its final resting place. My sister has always been very strong. The installation of the pipe was already proceeding, and she believed that Martin Briley would never be found there. She reopened a portion of the trench where work had already been completed, and placed him there. I'm told that something in the soil has preserved him. I can only say I am grateful that I don't have to look upon him. At least not in this life.

"There are so many ways my sister's plan could have gone wrong. We could have been seen when we arrived at the village, or going to and from the mausoleum. We might have been questioned when she helped me into the house. She could have been discovered when she moved and buried the body.

"Later, perhaps some crony of Martin Briley's might have come down from London. We were careful to pay any of Martin's debts that appeared, before questions could be asked. Eventually, his London creditors must have been appeased, because we heard no more from them.

"I was careful never to go to London, so that I wouldn't run into anyone that either knew me from the old days, or any of Martin's dubious associates. As the years went by, I stayed here, although I would dearly have loved to get back there, and perhaps visit some of the locations memorialized in my favorite books. But the habit was ingrained by then, and there was always something to do here at home.

"When I first assumed Martin's place, I was especially worried that the villagers might recognize me, but they seemed to accept my new identity. Perhaps I had changed enough while I was gone that no one here knew me any longer. I had certainly never had any friends while I was growing up, and there was no real school then to attend. Possibly the locals were just happy to have someone at the estate who was interested in seeing to their welfare for a change, and they didn't question the situation too closely. In any case, I was careful to wear work gloves for a number of years until I was sure that my scar would pass unnoticed.

"The rest of my story passes quickly, as does a life when viewed from the wrong end. I assumed the role of Martin Briley, but I vowed that I would not live like he would have lived. I well remembered my experiences as a poor mistreated village boy, and I made every effort to improve the lives of those that fell within my sphere. I started the schools, and made improvements where I could, as you have probably heard. Often my sister opposed me, saying I was just wasting the money, but I had to do it. After all, how else could I justify what we had done, if not to do something good with it? I had built up a quantity of debt, and it had to be repaid, even if it took the rest of my life. And it has.

"I don't know how Martin Briley would have lived his life here, had he gotten the chance. I suspect that he would have been dead within a year, all on his own. But circumstances had placed me in a position to do some good, and so I tried to do so. I hadn't planned anyone's murder, but I had helped to conceal one, and I must try to make amends.

"Of course, my sister never married. She has been content to live in this house, under the title of housekeeper, as if it were her own. And in a way, it has been. She paid a dear price for it, even more than I did. I believe she paid her very soul. Well, we are both old now, and we will soon find out.

"I expected that I would remain as alone as she, devoting my life to what service I could find around here. But then I met George's mother, and life changed for me.

"It was not long after she was widowed. She was a seamstress in the village, and I was riding by one night in a storm when I was thrown from my horse. She saw what happened and took me in. That night, there was just an innocent conversation lasting only a few minutes. But my heart was touched in a way that had never happened before. I found excuses to return, always being very discreet, and before long I knew she also loved me. However, she quickly determined that she was bearing my child. Of that, there was no doubt.

"I wanted to marry her then. She would not, stating that the village would be able to work out the truth of her shame in the matter. I offered to run away with her, leave everything, including the debt that I had taken on, in order to go somewhere that we could start new lives, but she wouldn't hear of it. She would not let me leave my responsibilities here. She gave everyone to understand that she was carrying the child of her recently deceased husband. She refused to have any further dealings with me, claiming it was for the best. I believe now that, at the bottom of it all, she was too ashamed of dishonoring her late husband's memory to ever allow us to be together. Completely inexperienced in the ways of the heart, I retreated to this house, a heartbroken man. And so, my son was born, while I sat up here brooding, and going through the empty motions of my life.

"I followed the boy's progress, and made opportunities for both him and his mother as I could. When she suddenly died, I realized that I had still been hoping for some miraculous reconciliation, even after all those empty years. For days I kept to myself, afraid to even show the staff any of my complete and total grief. And then I emerged, informing my sister that I intended to take the boy in, even if I could not reveal to him that I was actually his father without shaming his mother's memory.

"My sister fought me, more than she ever did on any of the many instances when trying to convince me to stop spending money on the countryside. But I was adamant. I went and got him, and brought him back here, and there is not a day that goes by when I don't see his mother's beautiful face looking back at me from his.

"I think that I have been a good father to him, even if he does not know that I am. I have trained him to be a skillful manager, and a good man. Years ago, I placed several benches around the estate, where I could sit at the end of a day's work and think. Many have been the evenings when George was smaller, when he would sit with me on one of the benches, and lean against me for warmth as the sun dropped beneath the horizon. And my arm has curled around him, my own son, and I have felt fulfilled more than at any other time in my life.

"A couple of these benches are under special trees. Soon after I took over the estate, I planted three English elms at certain locations on the property. I placed them so that at some time or another, every day, I would see at least one of them from wherever I was working and be reminded of what I had helped my sister to do, and what my payment was. The trees

155

were in honor of the Brileys, an unspoken acknowledgement of what I was trying to accomplish with their resources. One of the trees was a specific memorial to the man I had replaced, planted where he was secretly buried. I didn't put a bench under that tree. As lovely as that spot is, I couldn't bear to sit that close to the body that I knew was hidden there. That was the tree George pulled down a few days ago without my knowledge, when he was repairing the pipe leading to the mere.

"The second memorial tree is down by the mausoleum, by a bench looking out over the farms. You cannot tell it now, but the top of that tree can be seen from here in the house on a clear day. The third tree was near the stone bridge, where I would see it whenever I went to the cottages, which used to be a daily occurrence. I understand that lightning struck it today, killing it. Perhaps it is a sign, now that everything has come crashing down. I had really come to believe the old crimes would not be discovered, not at this late date. I had hoped that my penance would have paid the price, but as the old saying goes, murder will out."

We were all quiet for a few moments, thinking about what had been said, and listening to the sounds of the wind. Lynch reached up, adjusted the filled glass slightly to a different position on the small table, and then let his hand rest gently on the book there.

Finally, Holmes said, "Thank you, Mr. Lynch, for an illuminating account of the history of the matter. You have filled in the gaps in my understanding quite adequately. Sadly, I've heard nothing that relieves me of my dilemma."

"Dilemma?" I asked. "Holmes, what can you mean?"

"I think that I understand, doctor," said Lynch. "Mr. Holmes does not know whether or not to reveal the truth to the authorities. Am I correct?"

Holmes nodded. "Indeed. There is no doubt that you have performed a lifetime of good service here in the village, paying your 'quantity of debt,' as Mr. Dickens put it in your favorite book."

Lynch's eyes widened, as he realized that Holmes had indeed recognized where the quote originated. "If it were just you that still survived," said Holmes, "I would not be facing such a decision. But there is still a murderer who profits from what she has done, possibly a murderer several times over, and I do not think that even your years of penance can satisfy justice. And yet, if I reveal the truth about your sister, it cannot fail but to undo the work that you yourself have done.

"If it is revealed that you are not Martin Briley, the estate will pass from your control. Your careful plan to groom George Burton, who is a good man and suited for the position, will fail, and the estate will be broken up into whatever manner the courts see fit. An heir to the Brileys will be found, no matter how distant, and quite possibly inappropriate, such a person turns out to be. And this village, and its schools, and the workers and families who are tied to it, may all be hurt."

Holmes turned and paced a step or two, before shifting back toward Lynch. "I, too, have a quantity of debt. To myself. I want to believe that it would be better to allow you to live out the rest of your life doing good, rather than undo all that you have accomplished. Exposing you would exact a heavy price. And yet, there is the question of your sister."

"We, my sister and I, are both old now, Mr. Holmes," said Lynch. "These things have a way of taking care of themselves."

Holmes looked at him silently for a long moment. Then, Lynch tapped the book beside him and said, "I can tell from some of your perceptive comments that you must have read and know the works of Dickens, Mr. Holmes."

This apparent *non sequitur* seemed to take Holmes aback for just a moment. "In spite of Doctor Watson's early assessment of my limits, in which he stated that my knowledge of literature was 'nil,' I do have a passing acquaintance with one of our greatest writers."

"And you know *Great Expectations*? I must confess, the works of Dickens have been my particular favorites over the years, but this book has been of special comfort to me, as you will have perceived. I believe that you can understand why."

"Hmm. The story of a boy who rises from his humble beginnings to a better life," answered Holmes.

"And perhaps," I added, "the similar parallel of Burton being raised to a higher position, as was Pip, because his benefactor is actually a criminal."

Lynch seemed to wince slightly at my description, but he nodded. "There is another quote in the book that has always meant a great deal to me. 'I have been bent and broken, but — I hope — into a better shape.' "

Holmes replied, "I, too, recall a different passage in the volume which I have found applicable. 'Take nothing on its looks; take everything on evidence. There's no better rule.' "

Lynch nodded in agreement. "You do not disappoint, Mr. Holmes. And I would hope that the evidence that you have seen, and what I've tried to do with my bent and broken life, and the better shape that I tried to accomplish, would be enough."

"But Holmes," I interrupted. "We cannot allow a murderer to go unpunished!" I cried. "I agree that Lynch has worked for a lifetime to make up his part of the debt, and there is little doubt that if the Briley family had continued to run the estate, the lives of countless people would not be as well off as they are now. And yet, there must be a way — we must *find* a way — to punish the wicked!."

The door to the hall flew open at this statement, and Mrs. Lynch, who had obviously been listening for some unknown length of time, stepped in. "Wicked?" she cried. The flickering fire light only served to illuminate the madness flashing in the deadly eyes of the old woman advancing upon us. "You dare to call me *wicked*? I *saw* wickedness! I was *touched* by wickedness! The wicked have already *been* punished!"

Chapter 13 – Bent and Broken

"Sister," said Lynch, rising unsteadily from his chair. "Elizabeth," he said, in a softer tone. Then he nearly sagged for a moment, and I started toward his side, but he straightened and waved me back. His sister, also seeing his momentary failure, seemed to forget her rage for an instant, and a look of concern crossed her features. It occurred to me that she had been taking care of him, one way or another, for his whole life, and the small matter of being revealed to be a murderer, probably three times over, if not more, was not enough to turn her from her path.

She took several steps toward him before stopping, separated from him now by only a few feet. She was still dressed in the same dark clothing as earlier in the day, and she had obviously not been to bed. Seeing that Lynch was all right, she turned a glance toward Holmes, and then me. As her earlier rage quickly returned, her breathing became more ragged, and the whites of her eyes were quite visible as she looked back and forth from her brother to the both of us, standing to her right.

"What have you done?" she hissed at Lynch, taking another step toward him. "What have you told them? They never needed to know *anything*. It was fifty years ago! No one would ever have been able to figure it out!"

She rocked in place for a second, as if the violence within her was seeking a place to escape. "Elizabeth," began Lynch, but she spoke over him, her sibilant tones stabbing like knives.

"I would have thought of a way to silence them," she said. "I just needed more time! I could have put something in their food." Lynch raised a shaking hand and covered his eyes.

She turned to Holmes and me, facing us straight on as her expression darkened even further, if that were possible. "I didn't do it just to have the house or the lands. You have to understand that. I could have had them anyway. I had the old

159

man wrapped around my finger. He wanted to *marry me!* My God, he believed that I wanted to marry him too. But he was *evil!* He was the devil himself. His poor wife had found that out on her own, years earlier, before I was ever here. It put her into an early grave. And his son was going to be the same way. I could tell. No, it wasn't about the house. It was more than that. I had to put a stop to it. I had to put a stop to him. To both of them, father *and* son. For what they had both done! For what they had both done *to me!*"

Her strained voice trailed into a thin shriek, which coincided with a loud clap of thunder, followed almost immediately by a flash of lightning. She began to shake, and then gave a great sob before relapsing into near silence, the only sound being a high, thin, keening sound, which would have been barely audible, even if the storm outside was not displaying such renewed violence. Her arms hung straight to her sides, and her shoulders were rounded and sagging. It was terrible to behold. But it only lasted for the briefest of moments, and then she stopped it, as if throwing a curtain shut against the daylight. As quick as that, her outburst was gone, and the same Mrs. Lynch of earlier in the day was with us again, albeit a Mrs. Lynch now teetering on the edge of a homicidal rage toward the two meddlesome visitors who had helped to reveal her secret.

Lynch took a step or two toward her, and folded her into his arms. She resisted at first, and it was as if he were trying to bend a tree with his puny grasp. Then, little by little, she leaned into him, almost imperceptibly. He guided her into the second chair, on the other side of the small table from where he had been sitting. Feeling the seat of the chair behind her knees, she finally collapsed without any resistance. Slowly the emotions of a moment ago returned, and her face contorted into a terrifying rictus of agony, and her eyes were squeezed shut as tears began to flow down her lined cheeks. She was muttering something now, but too low to understand.

Whatever it was, it seemed to be the same phrase, over and over again, until it ceased to sound like words at all.

Lynch reached for the glass on the table that I had filled for him earlier, when he seemed to be tearing himself apart while coughing. He had held the glass then for a while, before eventually setting it untouched upon the table. Now, he picked it up and held it to her lips. He was bent awkwardly, stroking her hair and murmuring to her softly, seeming finally to break the spell of grief and anger which held her. She took a sip of the liquid, and then another.

Pulling the glass away, Lynch turned slightly and refilled it, before bringing it back to her lips again. She drank it all at once this time, closing her eyes and grimacing as the burn of it moved down her throat. Lynch then filled the glass a third time, and placed it in his sister's hand. He had to grip her fingers around it for a moment before she seemed to comprehend that he wanted her to take it. Finally, she grasped and held it. While Lynch turned and filled the second glass, she took another sip, and then lowered her hand and the glass, now half empty, back to her lap. She continued to weep, but with less emotion than before.

Lynch moved over to his chair, turned and sat down with a sigh. He raised the glass to his lips and took the smallest of sips, before stating, "I expect that last bolt of lightning took out the third memorial tree, the one down by the mausoleum. It would only be fitting that now, here at the end, all three of them would go down. The first when the body was found, and then the second by the bridge while you were investigating, and now the last." He coughed slightly, and winced in the slightest way. "Have you seen it? The tree by the mausoleum."

I nodded, and Holmes said, "Only in the darkness, I'm afraid. We were down there tonight, just before we returned to the house and began our chat with you.

Lynch raised his eyebrows. "You were down there? Down at the mausoleum? And did you go in?"

Holmes nodded, and Lynch continued. "Well, I'm sure you needed to see for yourself whatever it was that you required in order to answer all of your questions. But it really was a wasted trip, you know. I was waiting here, prepared for you. I had unlocked the terrace door in case getting past my sister in the house proved to be too difficult.

"As I said, I knew earlier today that you had figured out the truth. I thought that you would come in soon after dinner. I was prepared to speak with you, and then we would have summoned my sister." More softly, he said, "Instead, she found her way in here on her own. It has always been her way to take the initiative."

He glanced at Mrs. Lynch, who was holding the third glass of liquid loosely, and staring at the floor in front of her. She was starting to sag in the chair, and she hadn't made any attempt to drink any more from the glass.

Lynch started to raise his own glass back to his lips, and then he decided to speak instead. "There is a place in *Great Expectations*," he said, tapping a finger on the back of the green leather-bound book beside him, "when Pip says, 'In a word, I was too cowardly to do what I knew to be right as I had been too cowardly to avoid doing what I knew to be wrong.' That day, many years ago, when my sister committed a murder in front of my very eyes, I was a coward. I would like to think that tonight, I have finally been able to do what had to be done."

Holmes was watching him intently. Suddenly, I understood why. And, God help me, I simply watched as well, as Lynch raised his glass and drank the rest of the contents.

Beside him, his sister had seemed to settle lower in her seat. Her fingers opened, and the glass that she had loosely grasped dropped from her hand, fell, and rolled away, spilling the last unconsumed drops onto the fine rug beneath her. She made a small moan, and my trance was broken as I rushed to her side. A quick examination revealed the truth. "She's dead, Holmes," I whispered.

I stood and took a step back. Lynch was setting his glass onto the small table, obviously taking care to avoid looking at his sister. He then picked up his copy of *Great Expectations* from the tabletop and grasped it to his chest with his thin fingers. "You will have noticed, Mr. Holmes," he said, "that this volume contains two bookmarks." He tilted the book, so that we could see both of the envelopes pressed within it. "This evening, while I waited for you and Dr. Watson to arrive, I wrote a couple of documents, now here in this book. Since then, I have been revisiting some of my favorite passages."

He winced again, and then made a sharp little gasp, as if he had been pricked with a pin. I could see that even with only one glass of the liquid in him, unlike the nearly three that he had given to his sister, he was not long for this world. "One of these envelopes contains my will. It names my son, George, as my heir. I will tell you that the document does *not* explain that I am his father. As much as I have wanted to tell him the truth, it is now too late, and it would be far too terrible a burden to reveal to him at this point, and tell him that everything he has believed has been a lie.

"The other envelope contains a complete confession of the events that we have discussed tonight, signed and dated. I have been careful to explain everything, with no attempt at making any excuses whatsoever. It is a fair and balanced account, and should it be read, it will no doubt relate all the facts to whomever reads it, including whichever distant Briley relation that is found to take over the estate.

"I leave it to you, Mr. Holmes, and to you too, Dr. Watson, to decide what to do. Throw one or the other — or both or neither! I shall be beyond caring soon — into the fire. In moments it won't matter to me one way or the other." He coughed, louder this time, and twisted to the side in the chair, trying to find some relief.

Holmes said nothing for a moment. Then stepping forward, he leaned toward the dying man, making sure that Lynch could see him. "You should know what George is doing tonight."

163

Lynch, whose gaze was already fading, pulled himself back for a moment and focused on Holmes. "What?" he said. "What is George doing?"

"He has arranged to be married. On this very night, to Lydia Woods. He has been considering it for quite a while, as you know. It is also common knowledge in the village, where I talked to several people who knew about it. Her family knows, including her brother. Your sister had been becoming ever more objectionable about George's feelings toward the girl, not wanting your heir to marry a simple maid. George believed that Mrs. Lynch was eventually going to do something to irretrievably complicate matters if things kept going on as they have been.

"Finally, I took him aside tonight and revealed that I suspected his plans, and encouraged him to go ahead. It would serve to keep him out of the house, should he find a reason to interrupt our investigation and subsequent conversation. And at the very least, he needed to cement his happiness in case tonight's outcome should have any unpleasant ramifications.

"He did not want to do it without you. He agonized over the decision before I finally convinced him. Earlier, Watson and I saw him driving the carriage with Lydia inside, on their way to meet the minister, with whom he had earlier made arrangements. He intends to return here in the morning to surprise you with the happy news."

Lynch smiled, a forced and hideous smile, considering the pain that he seemed to be suffering, but a sincere smile nonetheless. "George married. I'm very glad to hear it. Very glad indeed." He roused himself one last time, and looked up at Holmes. "It is something else, then, for you to take into your considerations, Mr. Holmes," he said.

Lynch held Holmes's eyes for a moment, than weakly raised his right hand. Holmes, sensing the unspoken question, took a step forward and clasped it, shaking it now when he had declined to do so earlier. Then, Lynch released his grip and rested his head on the back of the chair, closing his eyes.

Folding both hands around the old book, he breathed, "Decide well, Mr. Holmes." Then, with a sigh, his soul passed from his body and he entered eternity.

We were left with the sound of the crackling fire and the terrible storm passing without. After what seemed like several long moments, I breathed softly, "My God."

Holmes, who had been as silent as I, seemed to return to himself. "Yes," he replied softly. He swallowed, and said again, with slightly more volume, "Yes."

He stepped forward and, raising a hand, closed the old man's eyes. Then, after a slight hesitation, he pulled the book from Lynch's hands. Letting it fall open, he retrieved the two envelopes, one labeled "Last Will and Testament" and the other marked "My Confession." He started to shut the book, and then shifted it closer to his eyes as he studied something with renewed focus. Then he glanced at me, and said, "There is a marked passage. Shall I read it aloud?"

I nodded, and he began. " 'That was a memorable day to me, for it made great changes in me. But it is the same with any life. Imagine one selected day struck out of it, and think how different its course would have been. Pause you who read this, and think for a moment of the long chain of iron or gold, of thorns or flowers, that would never have bound you, but for the formation of the first link on one memorable day.' "

He stood silently as we both thought of the words, and how they related to the life of Peter Lynch and that day so long ago when he had returned home at his sister's request, only to find that fate had thrust him onto a most unimaginable path. Certainly he had pondered that one unique day a number of times, and the marked passage in his favorite book had certainly resonated all the more for him.

But surely, I thought, it is the same with anyone, as was the point of the author. The day Martin Briley had returned home had been such a day for him, when his destiny was altered. Or when the Lynches' father had brought his family to Bedfordshire. Or when old Galton Briley had allowed

Elizabeth Lynch into his house as a scullery maid. Was that the day that had forged the first links in the long chain of events leading to the deaths of the two old siblings in front of us? Truly, everyone could look back at a hundred days, nay a thousand, in his or her own life and find where a different path was taken than the one that had been expected or hoped for. And yet, not all paths followed the route of the one that fate had laid out for Peter Lynch, known now for nearly a half-century as Martin Briley.

Holmes may have been thinking some of the same thoughts. His gaze was quite far away, and then he seemed to bring his focus back to the scene in front of us. He closed the book, and then opened one of the unsealed envelopes and pulled out a couple of sheets, covered in even, old-fashioned copperplate. He read for a moment, and then passed the pages to me. "The will," he said, unnecessarily. He was apparently more shaken than I had believed. I glanced at it quickly, and then reread it more slowly. It did not take long.

"Everything to George Burton," I said. "With no other explanation of any sort."

"It seems to be completely legal," said Holmes.

"And the confession?" I asked, nodding toward the other envelope. Without a word, Holmes removed it and started reading, passing each page to me as he completed it. There were considerably more sheets than the two comprising the will, with each written in the same careful handwriting. It took us several long minutes to read the thing completely through. In the meantime, the two Lynches, brother and sister, both bound in death as in life by their secrets, sat in their chairs, almost expectantly as if to see what our decision would be.

Finally, I finished the last sheet and handed it back to Holmes. He folded it neatly with the rest of the confession, and placed it back in its own envelope. "Written exactly as he told it," Holmes said. "I see no reason to doubt its veracity."

"Neither do I."

"Then — ?" asked Holmes, holding up both of the envelopes, his eyebrows raised.

I nodded toward one of them, and Holmes agreed. He tucked that one back into the green book, and then stepped to the fireplace. He leaned down and carefully placed the other envelope onto the coals, making sure that it did not fall behind the grate for possible later discovery. We had seen that sort of thing happen before. This was one document that we wanted to make certain had been destroyed.

We both watched as it began to spark around the edges, and then smoke and blacken. It took several minutes, during which time it seemed that it might not burn at all, but rather simply char and curl. However, it finally burst into flame, and in just a moment, it was fully ablaze. Holmes took the poker, and carefully broke up the remaining leaves into ash. The document was gone.

Holmes walked over and locked the outside door. Then he replaced the green leather book and the document that it held on the shelf, in the open space with the rest of the Dickens collection. He did not push it all the way in, but it was not obvious that it was pulled out, either. He and I retrieved our coats and hats from the floor. We gave another look back at the two old figures sitting in their chairs, separated by the small table. Holmes frowned, and then seemed to reach a decision, saying, "Just one more thing."

He walked over to the table and picked up the bottle of unknown liquid, which we now knew to be a potent killer. He removed the stopper and cautiously sniffed, before shaking his head. "There is nothing that I can tell this way. There is no odor. Only a chemical test would reveal the truth." He stepped to the fireplace. "I don't suppose that it matters in any case. Probably Lynch obtained this and held it in reserve for quite a while, in the eventuality that he ended up requiring such a drastic solution."

He bent by the flames and poured some of the liquid onto the fire. It sizzled and steamed, and then it was gone. The fire quickly returned where the liquid had been poured. Holmes held up the bottle, and I could see that there were now only a few drops remaining. "It is enough for the police to analyze, if they so choose, but not enough to remain and cause further mischief."

He put the stopper back in the bottle and stepped to the small table, between the two bodies. Then he placed the bottle conspicuously on Mrs. Lynch's side of the table, instead of where it had previously rested by her brother. He took a moment to feel in the pocket of Lynch's dressing gown, before pulling out a key, which he proceeded to transfer to the pocket of Mrs. Lynch's dress. Then, seemingly satisfied, he rejoined me at the door, and we stepped softly into the hall.

The house was silent, and the sounds of the storm were muted this deep into the house. Pulling the door shut, Holmes retrieved his picklocks from a pocket, and then he bent and locked the door.

We rehung our coats and hats where we had found them, and relocked the door to the terrace. Holmes motioned that I should precede him, and we crept upstairs to our rooms. There, we both found the same seats that we had occupied some hours earlier and sat down to smoke. There was no conversation. None was needed. We would not be sleeping this night, as we waited for the grim discovery to be made in the morning.

Chapter 14 – The New Day

Sometime around dawn, both Holmes and I roused ourselves from our respective chairs to prepare for the day. As I had expected, neither of us had slept. I had stopped smoking long before Holmes, of course. He often spent many a night with his pipe, wrestling with a problem until he had shaped it into a structure that he could comprehend. I suspect that often his "three-pipe problems" stretched until they were four, five, or even six pipes.

The storm had ended during the early hours of the morning, and when the sun rose, it revealed a bright spring day, washed clean and alive. Even from our window, I could see that the gardens and flower beds close to the house showed fresh new growth. The window was on the side of the house facing in the direction of the cottages. Down the long slope in that direction, it was obvious that the stream was up, and part of the old bridge was under water, cutting off the collection of tiny homes from the rest of the estate.

Beside it, caught in the muddy water and forcing it to swirl as it flowed past, was the shattered wreckage of one of the elms that Peter Lynch had planted as a memorial and a reminder to himself. MacDonald's description of the night before had been accurate. It looked as if the lightning had caused the upper portions of the tree to explode.

As I turned away from the window, one of the maids brought in hot water. She was surprised, I think, to find us already up. It occurred to Holmes to turn down and muss the beds, so as to appear that we had actually slept. After a shave and a fresh shirt and collar, I felt ready to face what we both knew was coming. Holmes managed to look refreshed, as he had always displayed a certain cat-like cleanliness, except on those many occasions when he was forced to undertake a filthy disguise. Except for some circles under his eyes, giving them a

169

slight bruised look, one would never believe that he had been up all night. I was certain that I did not look nearly so well.

We eventually started down to breakfast. Before reaching the stairs, Holmes pulled me over to one of the back windows, looking out on the rear grounds of the house. I could see the slope that we had traversed in the darkness the night before, the narrow track passing from left to right, and the copse where we had momentarily hidden while Burton's carriage had passed us. Past the track was the mausoleum, shining brightly in the clear morning light. Beside it was the wreckage of a great tree, destroyed in the storm. It looked as if it had been struck in the middle by lightning. As the top half had fallen away, part of it had remained attached to the trunk below, pulling the whole thing out of the waterlogged ground. It had fallen, just missing the mausoleum, but completely destroying the marble bench beside it. One of the same marble benches, according to Peter Lynch, that he and his son had used.

"He was right," Holmes said softly. "The storm did take the third and final tree, there at the end of it all."

We made our way downstairs, and Holmes contrived to lead us by the room where Lynch and his sister were waiting to be discovered. So far, the door was undisturbed, and we passed on into the dining room, where we found that breakfast had been laid.

Several of the servants were whispering as we served ourselves, and I gathered that they were puzzled by Mrs. Lynch's absence, along with Lydia's. I made an effort to appear oblivious to their huddled conversations, instead concentrating on eating my breakfast. Holmes had also gotten some food, and he ate it with machine-like precision. I almost believe that he only ate so that the servants clearing the table would not have reason to comment on the guest who partook of nothing, which might have seemed suspicious in some way.

We had nearly finished that joyless meal when there was a commotion at the front of the house. Before we could rise and determine its source, we heard quick footsteps coming down the hallway to the dining room. Turning in my chair, I was in time to see a beaming George Burton enter, with his glowing bride clinging to his arm. I reminded myself that I was supposed to know nothing of the tragedy waiting to be discovered across the hall, and of how I should react when I heard Burton's good news.

"We did it, Mr. Holmes! We were married last night!" One of the serving girls clearing the table audibly gasped, and Lydia looked her way. Their eyes locked, and Lydia smiled, dimples appearing on her cheeks. The young maid could not help herself, and a smile also broke on her face. Setting down the dishes, she dashed from the room to the back of the house, barely able to contain herself. We could hear her calling the news to the staff before she ever reached them.

Holmes and I moved around the table, offering our most sincere congratulations. I was happy for Burton, and glad that Holmes had encouraged him to go ahead and wed his true love. She would give him strength for the trial that was lying ahead of them both.

Burton was still explaining the events of the night before, how he had arranged with the local clergyman to perform the ceremony after having gotten the license weeks earlier, and how he had put Lydia into the closed carriage and driven her from the cottages, where she lived with her parents, and over the bridge, which was even then starting to flood. They had gone on to the church, where they were married before Lydia's parents, who had arrived ahead of time to make preparations, and their friends in the village. His only regret, said Burton, was that his protector and mentor, Mr. Martin Briley, had not been able to attend. However, he knew that the old man was too ill, and the wedding could not wait any longer. He was sure that Mr. Briley would understand. Holmes glanced at me quickly, and then away, before we might give anything away.

While we were still talking with the Burton newlyweds, we heard the front door open and close. There were muted conversations in the front hall, and then footsteps, as Woods led Inspector MacDonald into our presence. Woods was beaming, and he caught his sister's eye, and then mine, before he turned and left the room.

"I took the early train," he said, looking at us all, one at a time. His gaze lingered on the Burtons, and especially young Lydia's tight grip on her new husband's arm. "And have I missed something?" he asked.

Burton quickly explained that he and Lydia had gotten married the night before. I could see that his natural policeman's suspicions were aroused, but he seemed to accept that Burton had simply been driven to wed his bride by Mrs. Lynch's constant interfering, and the belief that she might do something to cause more trouble if matters were not taken in hand.

At the mention of Mrs. Lynch's name, one of the girls stepped forward hesitantly, and said, "Excuse me, gentlemen? And . . . and . . . Mrs. Burton," she said hesitantly, with the hint of a small giggle. Lydia beamed back at her. "About Mrs. Lynch. It seems that . . . well, we can't *find her,*" the girl blurted out. "We've looked everywhere. She's always the first one up, but not today. She didn't answer any of the knocks at her room, and finally Polly was brave enough to open the door. Her bed hasn't been slept in. There's only one place left to look.

"We already tried it, and the door to Mr. Briley's room is locked. We can't check in there," she continued, rather helplessly. "Usually Mrs. Lynch takes care of the master, with our help, but today no one has been in there. There is no answer when we knock, and the door is locked," she repeated. "That door is never locked. We even tried to see in from the outside windows, but the curtains are blocking our view. I hate to ask, but . . . Mr. Burton? Sirs? Can you check to see if Mrs. Lynch is in there with Mr. Briley?"

There is little need to elaborate on what happened next. A key was eventually found for the door, after some little trouble. Holmes made no effort to offer the use of his skills or his lock-picking devices. Finally the door was opened, and the bodies of the two old people were found. Burton had previously sent his wife to wait with the staff, but she was called back to her husband's side when he had to be led away after seeing the silent remains of the closest thing to a father that he'd ever had.

Holmes made cursory glances around the room, but left most of the inspection to MacDonald. The Inspector spent a long time looking at the two figures by the fire, now long since burned out. Finally, he said, "What do you think, Mr. Holmes?" He gestured toward the table, the two glasses, and the bottle beside the old housekeeper. Holmes, who had given the arrangement a passing look when we entered the room, was then over by the desk.

"Hmm?" he asked, his hand pushed into an open drawer.

"What do you mean?"

"The glasses, of course," said MacDonald. "Do you think that it's poison?"

"Oh, certainly," replied Holmes in an off-hand manner. "I should certainly have it tested, but I would expect that it is a quick-acting alkaloid, probably derived from the juice of a berry or plant, and easily disguised in the liquor."

"But what of the placement of the bottle?" MacDonald said. "Do you agree that Mrs. Lynch has done this thing? She had the key to the room in her pocket, indicating that she was the one who locked the door. The bottle is clearly on her side of the table. It seems obvious she must have poured something for old Mr. Briley, and then when he had drunk it, she poured one for herself, set the bottle on the table beside her, and drank hers off too."

"So it would appear," said Holmes.

"But why? Why would she kill him after all these years?"

"No doubt there was something about the discovery of the body in the trench that forced her hand," replied my friend. "We may never know at this point, nearly fifty years after the

173

original crime, exactly what happened, or what she feared might be revealed."

MacDonald eyed Holmes shrewdly. "It seems to me that you appear unnaturally disinterested, Mr. Holmes." He stepped closer to my friend, saying. "I've seen you crawl around the scene of a crime on your stomach looking for clues. You must admit that you barely glanced at the two corpses."

"It was obvious from the time that we walked into the room that the two had been poisoned, undoubtedly when one had the other drink unknowingly, and then the murderer also drank the deadly liquid. It was apparent that the bottle was by Mrs. Lynch. Thus, the conclusion must be that she did the deed, rather than Mr. Briley."

MacDonald continued to look at Holmes, who met his gaze without looking away. Finally, MacDonald looked back toward the bodies and said, "I spoke with your friend, Dean, last night. He confirmed that there are no other Briley heirs to speak of. The line is as moribund as can be imagined. This man here is truly the last of the Briley's."

He sighed, and continued, "There are absolutely no Briley heirs anywhere to be found. We might find a cousin thirteen-times removed, *if* we advertise from John o' Groats to Beachy Head, and *if* we bring in the Royal College of Arms to help us, but that would be the *only* way another Briley would be found."

"Dear me," said Holmes. "Then to whom shall the estate pass?"

"It will be up to the Crown, I expect," said MacDonald. He turned and walked over to the desk, where he shuffled half-heartedly through some of the papers there. Then, he turned back to us. "There was one other thing, however."

Holmes raised his eyebrows. "Really? And what would that be?"

"Before I departed from your friend, Dean, I thought to ask him if he'd heard of anything similar to this crime in Nimes, several decades ago."

174

"Indeed," replied Holmes. "And what did he say."

"He said it sounded familiar to him, but he couldn't recall the details."

"How unfortunate."

"But," added MacDonald, "he did recall where he could find them. It took him less than ten minutes. Interesting case, that." He waited for Holmes to inquire, but when nothing was forthcoming, he continued. "It seems that a body was found, hidden on an estate. It was discovered that it was actually the heir to the family fortune, murdered many years before. He had been killed by the man who had taken his place, living a life of luxury ever since."

"Ah, yes, now I recall some of the details," said Holmes.

"I'm sure that you do," said MacDonald, wryly. "The difference between that case and this one was that the man who took over the dead man's identity in Nimes was a true villain in every sense of the word. Quite a different man, according to Dean, than someone like poor Mr. Briley, here, for instance."

"Yes," said Holmes. "From all that we've heard, Mr. Briley spent a lifetime doing good works. The area will miss him greatly."

"That is true. It is unfortunate, indeed, that there is no will which might, for instance, pass on the estate to that fine young Mr. Burton."

"Hmm, yes, about that," said Holmes, turning away from MacDonald and toward the shelves. "I did notice something a moment ago. Now let me see . . . . "

He stepped to the section containing the green leather-bound books and peered closely at them, without touching them. Then, he said, "MacDonald, a moment, if you don't mind."

MacDonald joined him, but not before glancing my way with a gaze that suspiciously seemed to indicate that he was enjoying this game. "What is it, Mr. Holmes?"

"If you will observe, Mr. Mac, these are the Dickens books that we saw yesterday, when we interviewed Mr. Briley in this room. At the time, I pointed out that they seemed to be special favorites, as they were the only ones where there was no dust on the shelf."

"Yes, I recall it."

"I can assure you that when I looked at the books yesterday, all of them were pushed fully into the shelf. Now, as you can see, one of them is pulled slightly out."

"True," said MacDonald. "*Great Expectations.*"

"Exactly," said Holmes. "If you would do the honors?" he indicated.

MacDonald reached up and pulled out the book. He laid it flat on his large palm, and it fell open, revealing the envelope hidden within. "It's the will," he breathed. Then he looked startled for a second before his gaze shot toward Holmes. He started to say something, and then stopped himself.

We stepped over toward the desk. I was happy to let MacDonald precede me, since he didn't know what it said, while I did. Holmes reached across and lifted the envelope off the opened book. He pulled out the two handwritten sheets, and held them so MacDonald could read them over his shoulder.

"So the young man *does* inherit everything," MacDonald said. "No surprise, from what I've heard. And on the day after his wedding, too." Holmes handed MacDonald the will and the envelope. MacDonald looked at them, thoughtful for a moment, and then his natural suspicions took over. "You don't think that George Burton might have had something to do with this, do you?" He waved his arm back toward the bodies. "After all, the timing is quite fortuitous for him."

"Not at all," replied Holmes. "I'm sure that he was spending his wedding night at the inn, and it can easily be verified. No," he continued, nodding his head toward the bodies, "as you said, the evidence indicates that Mrs. Lynch did the deed, for whatever reason. We, all of us, may never know what happened here."

MacDonald walked back over to the chairs containing the old figures, placing the will in his coat pocket as he did so. He leaned down toward Lynch's body, reached out, and picked up the dead man's right hand. He turned it this way and that, examining the outer edge where the little finger should have been. Then, with a deep sigh, he let it drop back onto the dead man's lap.

Inspector MacDonald stood for the longest time, his arms akimbo on his hips. Finally, he shook his head and said, "I've known you for a while now, Mr. Holmes," he said, without facing us. "I want you to know that I trust you. I really do. Your wordplay of a moment ago, about *all of us* may never know the truth, did not pass unnoticed. You may be right that, for now, *all of us* might not know, but I hope that someday *all of us* will. In the meantime, I will continue to trust you."

He turned then, and looked at us, as we both waited expressionless as to what he was going to say. He gave another long sigh, and then a smile. "So, gentleman, and I think that you'll agree with me, this case is closed. And after all, what could anyone really expect us to discover about a fifty-year old mummy from the days of our grandparents, anyway? And regarding these other recent events, what has happened in this room is . . . unfortunate. But that's all it is. Unfortunate.

"But," he added, "I have the wee feeling that this could have been a very complicated mess indeed, more than I know. So I'm thankful for your presence here, Mr. Holmes. I'm certain that, somehow, I owe you a debt."

Holmes's eyes widened, almost imperceptibly, at MacDonald's unknowing word choice.

"And now," MacDonald said, moving toward the door, "shall we go see about arranging to have these people removed, and setting things right as fast as we can, so that new young family can get on with their lives?"

We took our leave soon after. MacDonald chose to stay behind, to tie up any loose ends. Before we departed, Burton managed to meet with us with his new bride at his side, in the sitting room, where he had told us his story the afternoon before. His grief was apparent, and it had only started to sink in that he was now the master of the estate.

"Thank you for coming down, Mr. Holmes," he said. "Inspector MacDonald told me how you found the will hidden in one of Mr. Briley's books. I'm — that is, *we* are in your debt. I can't begin to tell you how difficult matters would have been after his . . . his death, if the estate wasn't settled. I had come to believe that Mr. Briley was preparing me to take the place over after his death, but I was never certain. And I was not prepared for it to be this way, gaining the estate by the actions of Mrs. Lynch."

Holmes glanced my way, noting that I had also heard Burton's statement, which, in spite of his ignorance, was completely accurate. Burton now had the estate through Mrs. Lynch's long-ago efforts, when she placed her brother Peter in Martin Briley's place.

"It is certainly due to what she did that the estate has passed to you," Holmes agreed. "I'm sorry that we couldn't tell you more about the body that was found under the pipe. It has been my experience that some old secrets are never revealed."

MacDonald cleared his throat, but Burton did not appear to notice. It seemed to me that Holmes was walking a little too close to the edge with his cleverly ambiguous but truthful statements.

"Nevertheless," said Burton, "I am very grateful that you were here, if only because you convinced me that it was time to marry Lydia." His hand, which had enclosed her smaller one, seemed to hold tighter as he spoke. "I don't know how I would face this without her at my side." He paused to gain control of himself, and then said, "If there is ever anything that I can do for you . . . . "

"There is one thing that I would request, if it would not be too bold," said Holmes. After I heard what he wanted, I thought that *had* been too bold, and had asked for too much, but Burton did not seem to believe so. Perhaps, if he hadn't been in shock, he would have objected. In any case, he went and retrieved the item, which he placed into Holmes's hands. And then we departed.

Later, on the train back to London, I looked at Holmes, and he understood my unspoken question. "Lynch had taken it on himself to punish his sister, as a final act of courage to make up for his lack of it all those years ago, on the day that Martin Briley was murdered." he said, "He did it in his characteristic way, attempting to repay his quantity of debt by doing the deed so that he could take the blame. If I had left the bottle beside *him*, then MacDonald, and more importantly, young Burton, would have believed that Peter Lynch was the one who poured the final poisoned drink, and then we would have either had to reveal why he felt the need to do it, or left Burton with a doubt about the man who had been like a father to him, and in fact *was* his father. In the end, I did not want to have Lynch take that blame, in spite of the fact that it was true.

"Lynch knew as well as I did the choice that I faced. I could either let both him and his sister go, to live out the rest of their lives unpunished until old age took them, with their secret intact, or I could bring them both down together in order to serve justice. It is possible, perhaps even likely, that, if revealed, Mrs. Lynch might have taken all the blame to save her brother, but it was not certain.

"Lynch knew my dilemma. He had accomplished so much good over his lifetime, paying back his debt, and if it were revealed that he was *not* a Briley, all the effort that he had invested in order to train Burton to carry on his good works would have been wasted. Granted, the estate might have gone on just as successfully as before, but then again, it probably would not have. If nothing else, the story of the long-ago murder would have permanently attached itself to the place.

"I mentioned earlier that at times I've built up my own quantity of debt. Useful phrase, that. Lynch chose to assume the burden of the choice from me and take matters into his own hands as his final payment.

"But even after the deed was done, I did not want Mrs. Lynch to also get away blameless from that crime, as she had from the murder of Martin Briley, as well as her likely involvement in the deaths of Galton Briley and her own father. And who knows how many more there have been over the years, as she protected both the secret and also her brother?

"It is truly a tragedy, I suppose, that she felt forced into murder all those years ago, and who knows what evils she endured before she was driven to that point? But murder it was, or rather, murders they were, no matter the root causes. It took a lifetime, but in the end, she faced justice, at the hand of her brother."

We rode on in silence for a while longer. Despite the tragedy that we had just uncovered, into which we had been propelled only a day earlier, I felt somehow strangely renewed. Perhaps it was seeing how Lydia had already been such a source of strength for her new husband as he grieved for the old man — they would be fine. Or possibly it was simply looking out of the carriage window as the train rocked back to London, and seeing all of the new spring growth, shining in the mid-morning sun, and washed clean by the storms of recent days. In any case, my mood was one of careful optimism, and it felt as if it must be nurtured, like a tiny spark being encouraged into a flame, or perhaps more fitting on this beautiful spring day, like a tiny seedling into a flower. It was a strange feeling, because I still missed my dear Constance, but perhaps I was also starting to move on.

Holmes had been looking at the item which Burton had given him, just before we departed. It was Lynch's copy of *Great Expectations,* the worn green leather open across Holmes's lap. " 'Pause you who read this,' " he read, the underlined passage clearly marked in the bright morning sunlight spilling across the yellowed sheet, " 'and think for a moment of the long chain of iron or gold, of thorns or flowers, that would never have bound you, but for the formation of the first link on one memorable day.' "

He closed the book, and said, "So, are you still considering finding another practice, and moving out of Baker Street?"

I chuckled, and said, "Did you deduce that the question has been on my mind of late?" Before he could respond, I said, "Never mind. By this time, your powers do not surprise me any longer." Then I dropped my eyes as my amusement fell away, and I was silent for a while. Holmes sat quietly, patiently awaiting my answer. Finally, I replied, "Move out?" I cleared my throat, and said in a firmer voice, "No, I do not believe so."

There was more that I wanted to say. That I did not want to face the emptiness of another practice without my wife by my side, with the long hours of work broken by longer hours of loneliness until the next new day began. That I enjoyed the work that Holmes and I did, and found value and reward in it, and that I had finally come to understand that, even if my role was not luminous in and of itself, I could be a conductor of light. Perhaps most of all, I had my own quantity of debt to pay.

I did not realize at the time what the rest of that year would hold. We would meet many more people who needed Holmes's help, and he would provide it, with my assistance. I would continue to aid him in his ever-escalating battle with Professor Moriarty. That fall, I would meet Holmes's brother, Mycroft, for the first time. After the events at the Briley house, I was certain to notice that Mycroft and his brother Sherlock did, indeed, share the same type of ears.

Not long after meeting Mycroft, Holmes and I would become involved in the most trying and convoluted investigation our partnership would ever face, that of the Ripper Murders and the events ever after associated with the vile alleys of Whitechapel. Holmes and I had never faced a more serious crisis as that one, when that evil cabal of madmen united under the flag of death to terrorize a city. They worked together from all levels of society, threatening to engulf us. I cannot imagine any other way that the matter could have been resolved, except by Holmes and me, working in harness together. If I had been back in practice by that point, as I had considered just a day before, all might have been lost, including the British Empire!

But most importantly, that same autumn, I would meet someone who would heal my devastated heart. In the course of one of Holmes's investigations, I would encounter his client, the woman who would become my new wife, Mary Morstan. And if I had gone back into the lonely practice that I had been considering only a day before, I would have forged a completely different set of links on my chain, and my path and hers might never have crossed at all.

So my answer to Holmes, "I do not believe so," was the only reply that I gave. He nodded and took out his pipe. Really, nothing further needed to be said. He scratched a match and puffed until a comfortable flame was evenly burning across the tobacco. I shifted in my seat, and turned back toward the window. After a while, I was excited to see the outskirts of the great metropolis come rolling into view. We were nearly home. And with any luck, we would not have to wait long for our next adventure to begin.

About the Editor

David Marcum began his study of the lives of Sherlock Holmes and Dr. Watson as a boy in 1975 when, while trading with a friend to obtain Hardy Boys books, he received an abridged copy of *The Adventures of Sherlock Holmes*, thrown in as a last-minute and little-welcomed addition to the trade. Soon after, he saw *A Study in Terror* on television and began to search out other Holmes stories, both Canon and pastiche. He borrowed way ahead on his allowance and bought a copy of the Doubleday edition of *The Complete Sherlock Holmes* and started to discover the rest of the Canon that night. His parents gave him Baring-Gould's *Sherlock Holmes of Baker Street* for Christmas and his fate was sealed.

Since that time, he has been reading and collecting literally thousands of Holmes's cases in the form of short stories, novels, movies, radio and television episodes, scripts, comic books, unpublished manuscripts, and fan-fiction. In addition, he reads mysteries by numerous other authors, including those that he considers the classics, Nero Wolfe, Ellery Queen, Hercule Poirot, Perry Mason, and Holmes's logical heir, Solar Pons.

When not immersed in the activities of his childhood heroes, David is employed as a licensed civil engineer. He lives in Tennessee with his wife and son, and plans with great passion to finally travel one day to Baker Street in London, the location he most wants to visit in the whole world.

David is also the author of *The Papers of Sherlock Holmes,* Volumes I & II. Questions and comments may be addressed to:

thepapersofsherlockholmes@gmail.com

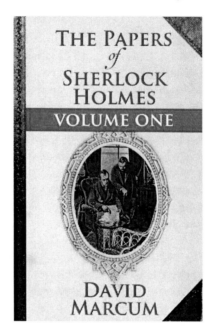

Also from MX Publishing

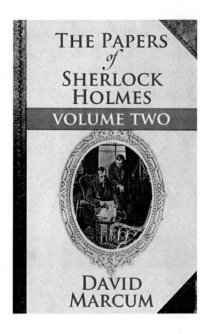

The Papers of Sherlock Holmes - Volume II

More traditional Sherlock Holmes stories from David Marcum.

MX Publishing is the world's leading Sherlock Holmes books publisher with over 100 titles.

www.mxpublishing.com

Also from MX Publishing

 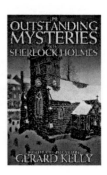

Also from MX Publishing

A Study in Regret

What if two had perished at Reichenbach Falls? One simple, disastrous error throws Sherlock Holmes from his intended Hiatus into a tortuous journey of sorrow and remorse. Far from home, broken in body and spirit, the haunted detective fights to survive the single most tragic failure of his career - a fight he cannot win alone.

www.mxpublishing.com

Also from MX Publishing

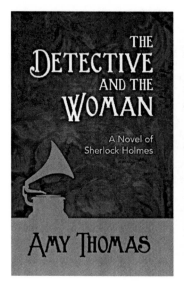
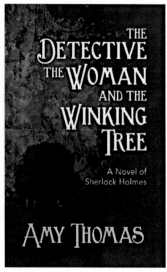

Two acclaimed novels featuring 'The Woman', Irene
Adler teaming up with Sherlock Holmes

www.mxpublishing.com

Links

MX Publishing are proud to support the Save Undershaw campaign – the campaign to save and restore Sir Arthur Conan Doyle's former home. Undershaw is where he brought Sherlock Holmes back to life, and should be preserved for future generations of Holmes fans.

Save Undershaw   www.saveundershaw.com

Sherlockology   www.sherlockology.com

MX Publishing   www.mxpublishing.com

You can read more about Sir Arthur Conan Doyle and Undershaw in Alistair Duncan's book (share of royalties to the Undershaw Preservation Trust) – An Entirely New Country and in the amazing compilation Sherlock's Home – The Empty House (all royalties to the Trust).

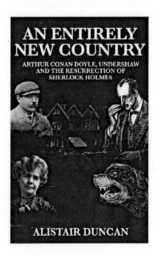

Lightning Source UK Ltd.
Milton Keynes UK
UKOW04n1528271013

219872UK00001BA/7/P